HONEYMOON
Hideaway

MIA LONDON

Honeymoon Hideaway

by Mia London

ISBN: 978-0983247470 (E-Book)
          978- 0983247487 (Paperback)

Publisher: Mia London Books™
PO Box 93852
Southlake, TX 76092
USA

Edited by Traci Hall
Formatted by Leigh Stone
Cover design by Just Write Creations

Published in the United States of America

To all my writer friends who are there,
supporting me, supporting one another.

Writing can be a lonely business, but you ladies
and gents make it wonderful.

A heartfelt thanks to all of you!

CHAPTER
One

After dancing with her girlfriends to Lady Gaga, Catherine collapsed into the wooden chair and gulped down half her ice water. Oops. That was her rum and coke.

"I don't know if I could be any happier for you, Cat." Celeste wrapped an arm around her and clinked her glass with Cat's.

Cat beamed. "Thanks, Cel. You're not just saying that because you're my maid of honor?"

"Nope," Celeste said, sending a little spray when pronouncing the "P". "Now, a toast. To the most beautiful bride in all of Travis County." Her blonde bestie lifted a shot of Bazooka Joe from the selection the waitress had just delivered.

All twelve reached for the fun blue drinks.

"Here, here," Bethany said, her big, almond-shaped eyes sparkling.

All Cat's friends plus her bridesmaids—Cel, Riley, Lori, Julie, and Bethany—joined in.

The concoction went down in a yummy stream—so good she'd lost count how many she'd had. Cat reached for her ice water, double-checking before she took a swig.

"Oh, my request! Let's go, girls." Lori popped out of her chair, her red curls bouncing in the process.

The beginning of "Jack & Diane" by John Mellencamp blasted over the speakers of the dance club/bar in downtown Austin. Cat's friends had planned the best bachelorette party a girl could ask for—the veil, the scavenger hunt, dinner, drinks at every bar. No detail left unnoticed. In fact, Riley had run into an ex-boyfriend and promised him a blow job in the back hall if he'd buy them a round. After he'd dropped off tequila shots, Riley's smile twinkled like her diamond-stud earrings, and she'd disappeared for a few minutes. Cat wished she could be as bold.

Cat wobbled when she stood and chuckled. Her fiancé's name was Jack, and her middle name was Diane—Catherine Diane. The tune was like their theme song.

Carving out space on the dance floor, the twelve women let loose. Arms flying, hair swinging, and voices shaking— they sang along. Cat pushed her play veil back into position.

A deep voice sounded behind her. "Can I help you with that?"

Cat spun around to find a sorta cute blond smiling down at her. He had a build similar to Jack, maybe a little taller, and his shoulder-length hair was tucked behind his ears. But his smile did nothing for Cat. When Jack smiled, butterflies took flight in her stomach. Every single time.

"Nope." She swayed, still fussing with her darn veil, and the blond put his hands on her hips to balance her.

"Sweetheart, you look like you're having all kinds of fun. Your groom is one lucky man. Mind if I dance with you?"

She grinned from ear to ear hearing reference to Jack. "He is." She nodded and felt a rush of dizziness again. "And you can dance with me, as long as you don't get any ideas."

He lifted his hands in surrender. "Promise."

They danced through the next three songs, and only twice did the blond need to grab her hips to stabilize her.

"I need water," she called to her girls and waved to the blond. Five of them followed her back to the table where she finished off her glass. She retrieved her phone from her mini purse to shoot off a text to her sweetie.

"What are you doing?" Celeste leaned in.

"Texting Jack."

"You really are smitten."

She looked up and sighed. "Celeste, how did I get so lucky? My world revolves around this man, and I couldn't be happier. Jack's different. I'm done with the losers." After about two years together, Cat had learned how caring and generous Jack was. He would always open the door for her and offer to pick up groceries from the store so she didn't have to shop.

Celeste grinned and sent her a wink.

She finished her text and reread it.

7

Hello my handsome fiancé. I'm having a wonderful time, but I'm thinking it could be even better if I dropped by tonight to do naughty things to you.

She giggled and hit send. Where did this gutsiness come from? The alcohol made her do it.

"Okay, next on the scavenger list," Lori announced as she unfolded the sheet of paper.

Her girls had made a list of things she had to do that night, like dance with a guy who was also named Jack, have a guy give her his underwear, kiss a bald man's head leaving a lipstick mark, and the list went on. She was about half-way through.

"Oh, you can do this one," Bethany pointed to number five: draw a tattoo on a bartender or bouncer.

Riley handed her a black marker from her purse while Cat scanned the room. The bartenders were slammed at the bar, and there wasn't a bouncer in sight, not that her double vision was reliable right then.

"Does a DJ count?"

The ladies looked at each other, silently taking a vote. "Yes," Celeste announced.

Cat carefully stood and made her way to the DJ booth. *Don't fall, and speak clearly.*

"Hey."

The DJ pulled his headset back from one ear. "Hey, pretty lady. Wanna hear a song?"

8

"No. I need to do a task."

"A task?" His eyes narrowed.

"Yeah. I have a list of things to do for my bachelorette party, and one of them is to draw a tattoo on the DJ." She wiggled the pen in her hand. "Will you let me?"

He stared at her for a beat. "What's your name?"

"Cat."

"Okay. Come up here."

She climbed the two steps as he held open the booth gate.

"Gimme a second." He put his headset back in place and pressed some buttons on his control panel. When the song ended, he clicked on the microphone. "Okay, you party fiends. In the house, we have Cat, our bride-to-be. Everyone give it up for Cat."

The crowd went wild with applause and hoots. Her girls beamed at her in the spotlight.

Geez! She hated the attention. *You can do this, Cat.*

"She has a list of things she needs to accomplish tonight. One is to draw a tattoo on the DJ."

Her smile fell. She hadn't thought about what she was going to draw.

"So, yours truly is going to be her willing-and-able victim." More hoots and hollers. "The question is, where do I get my tattoo? My arm? My stomach? Or maybe my ass?"

The crowd went positively wild.

Shit! He wouldn't. Holy crap!

"Now, calm down. I don't want to lose my job, so pretty lady, stomach it is." The DJ leaned forward to the control panel to play the instrumental piece from the Jeopardy game show. Then, he lifted his shirt to reveal a reasonably taut stomach with very little hair. "Okay, sweetheart, have at it."

Her brain couldn't fire on all cylinders. There was only one thing that came to her mind. "Here goes."

Cat knew the image well, although the marker didn't allow for much detail work, not like her charcoals. She took about two minutes and felt the DJ getting impatient. She finished quickly and wrote a caption.

The man tipped his head down to his stomach, and his mouth dropped open.

From the applause and laughter, the crowd seemed to love her work.

It wasn't her best by any means but with such limited time... She winked at her portrait of Jack, gave her thank you to the DJ, and returned to the table of her exuberant friends.

"Oh my god. You are crazy," Julie said.

"I can't believe you did that." Bethany shook her head and smiled.

"What did you write underneath?" Riley asked.

"*Jack 4 Ever.*"

The girls broke into laughter all over again.

The night ended around two, everyone hugging and piling into their Uber rides. Cat and Celeste's driver pulled up to Jack's apartment building.

"Are you sure he's home?" Celeste glanced up to the second floor.

"Not exactly. He didn't reply to my text," which was unlike Jack unless he was hip-deep in a major project, "but he didn't have plans tonight other than going to Randall's for the game. I'm sure he's sound asleep in his bed." She grinned, thinking about the delicious way she would wake him up. Although she'd never done anything as courageous as this before, she had his key and was prepared to use it.

"I'll wait here until I see you get inside." Celeste wasn't just a good roommate, she was her best friend. Cat's parents had almost divorced when Cat was fifteen, and Cel had gotten her through. All the years of experimental hair-dyeing? Cel at her side. And she'd been right there during the breakup with Weird Will, her boyfriend during college.

"Okay, sounds like a plan." Cat climbed the steps without issue, retrieved his key from her purse, and opened the apartment door.

Her heart raced in anticipation. She waved to Celeste in the waiting car, and Celeste waved back.

Cat stepped into Jack's dark apartment and quietly closed the door behind her. She loved spending time here, and couldn't wait to move in next week. The spaciousness of the hardwood floors and the new appliances in the kitchen were double the size of hers. Of course, Jack's job as a stock broker meant he could afford a big apartment like this.

She set her purse down, lifted her skirt, and slid off her

11

panties. She suppressed a laugh that threatened to bubble up. She'd thought a few times of doing something like this, and now, here she was. Two days before she was officially Mrs. John Sumners.

Licking her lips, she slowly made her way down the hall to his bedroom. Immediately she noticed a light spilling from the cracked doorway. He was awake.

Maybe he'd gotten in late too. Or maybe he'd fallen asleep with the light on.

No worries. He would still *love* her surprise.

Stepping to the door, her hand hovering over the knob, she stopped short. Was that a voice?

She pushed the door open just an inch or two and heard it again. This time with a moan.

Cat's breath hitched. He couldn't. He wouldn't.

She moved the door just enough to poke her head through, and nearly gasped. Her hand over her mouth silenced her shocked intake of breath as the scene played out before her. A naked woman in the center of Jack's bed on her hands and knees, a naked Jack pumping into her from behind.

Cat's stomach churned. Her fiancé was making love to another woman—a bleached-blonde with ginormous breasts.

Cat wanted to run. She wanted to scream. But she couldn't pull herself away. Like watching an accident on the road, she had to know what was going on.

Jack groaned, then pulled out of her.

"Oh baby, don't stop." The female's head dropped forward as she gasped for air.

"Don't you worry about that." Jack licked and bit her ass.

"Ooh, you know how I love that," the bimbo sighed.

Jack moved to her sex and practically buried his tongue in her.

Oh God. Cat stood stock-still, gaping, wondering how many times they'd done this. *He'd* done this, to this woman.

His fingers gripped her ass, separating her, and then... oh, he licked her, all the way up *there.*

The blonde moaned like a mare in labor. Jack hovered for several more beats before sticking his pinkie in her tiny hole.

Cat's muscles clenched.

This wasn't *her* Jack, it couldn't be. He never did these kinds of things with *her.*

Cat didn't know how much more she could take before vomiting. If she hadn't drunk so much, she would've slapped him—or something—by now.

He stood and entered her again, his hips and his pinkie working in concert.

The blonde pushed back on him and moaned.

"That's right, baby. Let me hear you," he said, preceded by a slap across her ass.

Cat gasped as if she herself had been slapped.

The two turned in her direction. Jack's mouth fell open. "Baby, you're here. I wasn't expecting you."

She stared hard at both of them. Neither looked away. *Say something.*

"I texted you." The words rolled off her tongue without a conscience thought.

Asshole. There was a thought. *What an asshole.* She was about to marry a certifiable, fucking cheating asshole.

"And who are you talking to, Jack? Isn't she *baby* too?" Cat pierced the air with her finger.

Jack pulled out of the woman on his bed. "No. Wait, let me explain."

"Asshole," she hissed. "You don't need to explain a thing. Your dick has done that for you." She quickly made her way to the living room, grabbed her purse and flew down the stairs, leaving the door wide open.

"Cat! Wait. I can explain," he yelled after her.

She didn't stop. She ran past the next building, across the parking lot, glancing briefly at a couple who tracked her flight. She didn't care what people thought. Gasping for air, fighting back hot tears, Cat dropped onto the bench outside an office and called Celeste.

"Can you come get me?" She gave her location and sobbed into her hands.

CHAPTER
Two

Cat awoke the next morning and froze as the memories of the prior night came rushing back. She groaned aloud. Wasn't there some way to fast forward through all this heartache, this embarrassment, to get to the part of "everything will be alright"?

A soft knock sounded before Celeste slowly opened her bedroom door and peeked inside. "How you doing?"

Her eyes felt sore and swollen, and her stomach was heavy as lead. "Shitty. What time is it?"

"About ten." Celeste walked in, holding a steaming mug. "I thought you could use some coffee, and here are two ibuprofen in case your head is pounding."

Not until she'd just mentioned it.

Cat grabbed the covers to hide her face and another ugly cry as tears threatened. "God, Celeste. What am I gonna do? Tomorrow is our wedding day. *Supposed* to be our wedding day."

Celeste sat on the bed and peeled back the sheet. Her

eyes filled with sympathy and love. "You're gonna do what you've always done when you're knocked down. Fight. One day at a time, you fight to get your life back, your sanity back."

Cat wiped her cheeks and sniffled.

"Don't worry about tomorrow. I can have the girls here in an hour if you want us to start calling guests and all that."

Cat nodded. "Did he come over?"

Celeste shook her head.

Why wouldn't he? Why wouldn't he fight for her? "Okay. Give me a few minutes."

Cel left, and Cat reached for her phone resting on the nightstand. The screen read thirty-eight missed calls and eleven messages, all from Jack. Should she dare to listen to the messages? What if he was sorry? *Oh please, does that matter?*

After a quick shower, Cat slipped on a pair of sweatpants and a cami, wrapped her wet hair in a bun on the top of her head, and dragged her body to the kitchen. Time to face the world.

Riley and Lori were already seated at the kitchen table, sipping coffee.

"Hi, sweetie." They both stood and wrapped her in a big hug. "How are you doing?"

"Lousy," she exhaled, "but I guess it's better that I know now, not after we got married."

16

"That's right," Riley nodded.

"I filled them in on what we need to do." Celeste joined the group at the table.

Cat looked down at her wedding binder. All her notes, guest list, contact information for the florist, caterer, church, reception hall, all of it was inside.

Celeste took her hand. "Are you sure this is what you want?"

Cat slumped into an empty chair, letting a few tears flow. She was among her close friends.

Lori handed her a tissue.

"I don't see how I can trust him again. I feel so... so destroyed. How is it a man can have that much power over me? I believed in him, in us. I gave him everything. I thought I was getting everything in return. Turns out I was just sharing him." More tears streamed down her cheeks. "And I feel embarrassed." She waved a hand over her year of work on planning for what she'd hoped would be the event of her life. "Now I get to make it public that I've been jilted."

"Oh, sweetie. Give it time. Don't think about all of this," Celeste implored. "We'll take care of it."

"How do you want to handle Jack?" Riley cupped a hand over hers.

She stared down at her phone. "I'm gonna call him."

"Okay. We'll take care of this," Celeste tapped her binder, "while you do that."

"Then we'll order in lunch and watch a comedy. How

does that sound?" Lori smiled meekly.

"'Kay. Thank you all for helping me. I don't know what I would do without my girls."

Celeste hugged her when she stood up. With her phone in hand, Cat went to her bedroom and closed the door.

With a deep breath, she pushed past the boulder in her gut, wiped her eyes, and made the call.

"Oh God, you're alright. I was so worried." Jack's voice sounded rough and tired. *Serves him right. And if he was so damn worried, why didn't he come over?*

"Jack—"

"Wait, before you start. Let me say how sorry I am. It was a moment of weakness, and I promise you, it will never happen again."

He sounded sincere, but was he sorry for cheating or sorry for getting caught?

She willed herself to be calm, even though her insides were torrents of emotion, wreaking havoc on her stomach, her mind, her heart. "I understand. Jack, let me ask you. How many moments of weakness have you had?"

The air over the phone deadened. She waited. She'd seen enough lawyers at her work question people, getting at the meat of the story. There was always more than what was disclosed.

"Well, I couldn't—"

"Take your best guess. You can be honest with me. With the blonde woman and anyone else as well."

Her throat constricted asking the question, fearing the answer, but she had to know. She didn't bother to wipe her tears since more would fall. She moved the phone away from her mouth and took a fortifying breath. *Keep it together, Cat.*

"It was the fourth time with Bonnie." His voice held a meek and pensive tone.

Shit! "The blonde from last night. But she's not the only one. How many have there been? Total?"

"Cat, you really don't want to know."

She swallowed hard, her eyes crushing closed as if it could stop the acid tears or the images of him with other women. "Yes, I do. I need to know, Jack. How many?"

"Eight," he said in barely a whisper.

Oh God. Oh God. How could he? What did I ever do to him?

She willed her brain to work, to hang on for a few more minutes. She had to get through this. Then she never had to talk to Jack again. "I see. Let me ask you one more question. If you wanted all of them, why propose to me?"

He sighed. "Cat, please let me come over. Let's discuss this in person."

She knew that wasn't a good idea. He would try some kind of manipulation, and she wasn't strong enough right now to handle it.

"We can talk over the phone. Why, Jack?" Her voice cracked.

"I don't know. They were more adventurous, I guess."

19

"Adventurous?" Her stomach triple-knotted. That hit a little too close to home.

"I love making love to you, but it always... it always seems so safe. So cautious. Like you were holding back. I guess I wasn't thinking straight. I wanted this with you, but since we didn't... God, Cat. I guess I thought I could sow my oats before we got married. Sorta get it out of my system."

Get it out of your system? What an asshole!

"I see." Tears streamed down like a running faucet. What more could she say? Her brain was locked up. All the emotion, all the hurt, froze her in place. She wanted so badly to crawl out of her body, out of this life, and escape. Escape the pain, escape the embarrassment for being rejected for not being enough.

"Cat, please let me come over."

"Jack, I've reached a decision. The wedding is off. You won't change, this I'm certain of. I will have someone bring your things to you. Please gather up my stuff," she sobbed out loud, "so my friends... can pick them up." She croaked the words.

"Cat, no, wait. I swear it won't happen again. We have too much love between us to throw it all away."

"We *had* love between us. I trusted you. That trust is broken and won't ever be repaired. Goodbye, Jack."

She hung up the phone and wailed. "Ah." She cried out, trying to release the misery.

The phone rang in her hand. Jack.

She just stared at it through clouded vision. When the device went silent, she opened her contacts, and hit "block". She was done trusting him, he was out of her life, what more was there to say? He could have his adventures; she'd be too busy trying to piece herself back together.

She staggered to her feet and rummaged through her drawers and closet. He'd mostly had shirts and underwear at her place. A pair of his running shoes sat in her closet. She shoved it all into a canvas bag and went to the bathroom. Toothbrush, deodorant, razor, cologne, and comb. Then, without more than five seconds of thought, she pulled the photographs of them out of her drawer and off her dresser. A year and a half of memories, erased in a heartbeat. But for her sanity, she knew this was what she had to do. She couldn't be surrounded with the memories of Jack anymore.

Looking down at the ring on her left hand, she slipped it off and set it in her jewelry box.

She strolled back to the living room. Her girls were busy on their phones. Cat gathered the photos from around the space of her and Jack, so many great times. Well, maybe someday she would appreciate them because now they all seemed like one big fat lie.

Eight women. For fuck's sake!

She dropped the bag by the front door, causing a thump. Then, she grabbed her key ring and wound Jack's apartment key off—tossing it on top.

Celeste finished a call and looked up at her. "How ya

doing?"

"Numb."

"That's to be expected. Want some more coffee?"

"Yeah. But I can get it."

A knock came at the door and she jumped, her heart lodged in her throat. She knew who it was. "I can't see him, Cel. Not now," she stage-whispered.

Celeste held up her hand. "I know. I'll handle it."

Cat peeked through the peep-hole and nodded, confirming it was Jack. Celeste pulled open the door. "What is it, Jack?"

"I need to see Cat."

"She doesn't want to see you right now. She'll call you when she's ready, *if* she's ready."

Cat heard him sigh.

"Please, just let me in."

"Face it, Jack. She's done. You took a gamble and lost. You had a fifty-fifty chance that you wouldn't get caught. Those odds are better than Vegas. But you lost. Time to cash in your remaining chips and go home."

Cat heard nothing more from Jack. Celeste just stared straight ahead, letting him know she was not backing down.

God, she loved her friend so much right then.

"Oh." Celeste leaned down to pick up the canvas bag. "She wanted me to give this to you." Cel swung the bag backward and sent it sailing. It made direct contact with his privates.

He doubled over. "Ow."

Cel grinned as she closed and locked the door.

Tears filled Cat's eyes even as her mouth gaped. "Ohmigosh."

Celeste took her in a hug. "You're welcome. Remember—one day at a time."

She nodded, secretly glad that Cel had used Jack's balls as target practice.

The day proceeded without any further incident. She made a call to her parents, who were incredibly supportive. She promised to phone them later when she was alone. The girls sat around the living room, eating pizza, drinking a little beer—after the previous night, everyone was cautious—and watching some comedy of which Cat could barely recount the storyline. Instead, her mind replayed every date, every conversation, every time she'd made love to Jack, and questions filled her head. What did she do? What didn't she do? What could she have done better? Oh yeah, be more adventurous. Well, she already knew that. Shit, *he* already knew that too. He'd never once complained about her lack of *adventure*. What a fucker!

He'd said something once, like *wouldn't it be cool to try this outside sometime?* Or that time he'd tried to get her to go out to dinner with a bunch of their friends and not wear panties under her dress.

Whatever. That was no excuse to sleep with all those women.

The day stretched as long as it could for Cat and she needed to bring it to an end. After the movie, she rose. "I'm going to bed, guys. I feel exhausted."

Celeste stood by her side. "We got everything taken care of, babe. Sleep as long as you need. There's only one thing we need to talk about, but it can wait."

What? Her shoulders slumped. *No more. Please let this nightmare end.* "Thanks. Goodnight, guys."

"Goodnight, Cat." They hugged her, and she went to her bedroom.

To her surprise, Cat fell asleep quickly. Unfortunately, she didn't stay asleep. No, she wasn't that lucky.

Feeling sad and depressed, she did what the experts would probably advise against—she opened her phone. The one place she hadn't gotten rid of the photos, and there were so many. Countless shots of selfies, some of just him, others where someone else had taken their picture.

Tears streamed from her swollen eyes, landing on her pillow.

How could she have been so blind? Jack was her everything. She'd thought of traveling together, buying a house, having kids, growing old. And he'd pissed it all away because *she* wasn't adventurous enough.

A sob escaped. She couldn't help if that was her nature. Her mother wouldn't exactly be described as adventurous, and her parents were happily married for over thirty years—

24

even through the rough patches.

Cat threw back the covers and meandered to the kitchen to make a cup of tea. The apartment was dark except for moonlight coming through the sliding glass door in the living room.

When her water was hot, she poured it over the tea bag in her cup and brought it out to her small patio. There was space for two chairs, a little table, and two potted plants. She sat and stared at the nighttime landscape from her sixth-floor apartment. Mostly dark houses, illuminated street lights, and the Austin skyline in the distance. The summer air was still and quiet.

She sighed over her cup. How could a person be more adventurous if that wasn't in their nature? Could a person change just like that? Could she?

She was obsessing, playing and replaying times when maybe she could have taken a risk, but didn't. The mental hamster wheel she was on exhausted her.

She heard a noise and turned around. Celeste stood at the doorway in the living room.

"Hey. Couldn't sleep?"

"Nope."

Celeste sat beside her. "Whatcha thinking about?"

"Everything." She looked at her friend. "Eight women, Cel! Who does that? He said he was sowing his oats with adventurous women. What a bunch of crap. I would have been more understanding if he was drunk, macking down with someone." She huffed. "Possibly."

Celeste's eyes softened. "I don't understand it either. Did he mention wanting to be more adventurous with you before?"

She shrugged a shoulder. "A few times."

"And that scares you."

She nodded. Honestly, it terrified her, but she also saw how exciting trying something new could be too.

"I don't know, Cel. I just feel fooled. *I* was a fool."

Celeste leaned in, her hand resting on hers. "Now don't say that. No one saw that coming. I thought you two were perfect for each other."

"Yeah." Well, whatever Celeste thought, she felt like an idiot. She didn't know how long it would be before she could trust a man again.

"Listen, there was only one thing we couldn't take care of."

Cat faced Celeste. "What is it?"

"The honeymoon."

"Shit," she said under her breath.

"Everything is paid for, and I can't get you any refunds. I didn't see anything about insurance. Did you happen to buy any?"

"No." She sighed. "I was expecting to go without any issues."

"I know. Well, I want you to think about something."

She stared at her friend.

"Go."

"What?" Her nose crinkled.

"I want you to go. You already have off work. It's paid for. And it will do you so much good."

She turned back to her skyline view. "I don't know about that. Come with me."

Celeste gave a small smile. "I can't take off right now. You can do this. Saint Lucia is beautiful. You've always wanted to go. You'll be at an all-inclusive or have guided tours, so you'll be safe going by yourself. *And...*" Celeste waited for her to look her way, "you can take your charcoals and have a little 'me' time. You know how drawing always helps soothe you."

Her charcoals. She'd been so busy with wedding stuff, she hadn't created any art in *months*. "I don't know, Cel. It sounds so cliché."

"Not cliché. Practical. Just think about it. Think about stepping out of your comfort zone. Your flight isn't until Sunday at two." With that, Celeste rose, kissed her on the top of her head, and went back inside.

Go by myself? On a trip that was supposed to be with my husband?

Cat would definitely need to sleep on that. Having a reminder that the trip was supposed to be her honeymoon thrown in her face didn't sound like her idea of a good time.

Cat finished her tea and went back to bed. Blessed sleep came as she reminded herself to take it one day at a time.

27

CHAPTER
Three

Saturday morning, Cat yanked off the covers and walked to the bathroom, stripping along the way. She had an energy, a determination, pulsing through her veins she hadn't felt before. Like some outside force was propelling her forward.

Frankly, she wanted to harness it, embrace it. This day was supposed to have been her wedding day, but if she dwelled on that, she'd be sick over Jack again. She was already tired of crying. Thinking about what could have been.

She dressed and headed out to the kitchen.

"Hey. How ya feeling?" Celeste looked up from her tablet and smiled.

"Strangely energized."

"Really?" Her friend's eyebrows rose.

Prepping a cup of coffee with cream and sugar, she said, "I need to get my gown and all that put away. I don't exactly know what I'll do with it, but I don't want to toss it out. Then

I need to unpack what I packed to move into Jack's."

"Okay, I like that plan."

Cat sat at the table across from Celeste. "Then, I'll go through my suitcase and make sure I have everything I need for tomorrow."

Celeste gasped. "You're going to Saint Lucia." It wasn't a question.

A small smile appeared, the first since she'd caught Jack cheating on her. "That's right."

"What made you change your mind?"

Cat sipped her coffee. "Well, you."

Celeste sat straighter. "Me?"

"You encouraged me to spread my wings. Plus I decided some time alone would help me reassess and reevaluate. I think some sun would be good too."

Celeste bit her lip. "And I like the idea that it's the last thing Jack could do for you—a free two-week vacation. I think he owes you that."

She grinned from ear to ear. "I one-hundred percent agree."

Cat spent the day getting organized, packing for her trip, and trying not to think about Jack. She'd cried a few times, but searched deep down for the strength to get through the day. She welcomed the determination that pulsed through her, because if she let it, the sadness and depression of this whole fiasco would swallow her whole.

She stopped for lunch Celeste had made, turning on her phone to call her parents and tell them where she'd be for the next two weeks.

"Honey, I'm happy for you. I think a trip is a great idea," her mom said.

"Thanks. Did Jack call you?"

Her mom's voice dropped. "Yes, he did. He asked if I would talk to you. Of course, I told him if and when you were ready to talk, he would likely be the first to know."

Cat loved that her mom was in her corner, and not trying to somehow convince her that "men slip up" or some other line of crap. "Great. Thanks."

They wrapped up the conversation, and Cat turned off her phone. She had no interest in hearing from anyone about this whole incident. She needed time alone to process.

Celeste pulled her out of her wandering thoughts. "Hey, care to go through your bachelorette gifts? You might even want to pack some of the gifts for Saint Lucia."

A distraction sounded like a banner idea. "Okay."

Celeste set the gifts on the table and grabbed a note pad to mark everything down.

The first gift was from Lori—a lavender bath and spa set. Cat knew she could relax with something like this. Next, Bethany had given her a purple satin robe with the word "Bride" in gold lettering printed on the back.

"Oops." Cel quickly folded it back into the bag.

The gifts continued—wine and chocolate, a jewelry box,

a luxurious sheet set. Then, she opened Celeste's gift—lingerie. She held up a bra that had a hole in each cup and matching panties.

"I love these cutouts, don't you?" Celeste said with a twinkle in her eye.

Cat wasn't much into fancy underwear, although the pink color was gorgeous.

Celeste cupped Cat's upper arm, and spoke softly, "This is a new chapter in your life, Cat. I know you feel like crap now, but it won't stay that way. Break out of the practical cotton bras and panties—because some day you will meet someone who will love to see you in this."

Cat groaned. She had no other response. She wasn't looking for a *someone*. She'd had a someone and he'd deceived her. There was no rush to fill the vacancy.

There was no use arguing so she reached for the next gift. Cat felt like she was having an out-of-body experience, like she was just going through the motions of life. She vacillated between anger and sadness, between energized to move on and depressed about what could have been.

She'd opened all her wonderful gifts—her friends were so thoughtful—when Cel patted the chocolate and lotions. "Do you want to check to make sure you have room in your suitcase for these?"

"Good idea."

By the time Cat had stuffed the last few things in her luggage, down to the sunblock and lip balm, Cel walked in holding her new lingerie.

"Don't forget this." She waved the garments in the air.

Again, not much Cat's cup of tea, unlike her BFF who had a passion for lacy and satin things. "No way, Cel. I'm not taking that with me."

"Aw, c'mon. It will make you feel sexy."

"That's okay. Maybe some other time." Cat's stomach rumbled. She considered that a good sign. "How about I make dinner tonight?"

"That works for me."

She was ever so thankful her friend dropped the subject.

Over spaghetti and meatballs, Celeste asked, "How are you feeling? Any phone calls?"

"I'm hanging in there. I don't know about the calls. I left my phone in my purse the whole day." She was doing all she could not to think about Jack or the wedding, but she didn't know exactly how to move on from something like this. There should be a manual or something.

"Are you still planning on going to Saint Lucia?"

The thought had crossed her mind a few times to bag it, but it never stuck. "Yes."

"Good. Are you thinking about calling him?"

"Hell no." Okay, that wasn't entirely true. She needed closure to heal, and she knew it...but would she actually get it from Jack, or would he feed her the same bullshit he'd dished out last time?

"Good and good. Be strong. One day at a time."

The seven and a half hour flight to the island of Saint Lucia was grueling. Not because of the length, but because Cat had serious second thoughts.

Who travels to some foreign place alone?

People do it all the time.

Sure, people who are more daring or brave.

She battled with herself, rehashed conversations with, not just Jack, but every boy she'd ever dated. Maybe those times she'd thought her relationships had simply fizzled because of lack of chemistry it had really been lack of risk-taking. Weird Will might have had some weird fetishes, but how could she *really* judge without trying and experiencing firsthand?

Never before had she felt so completely uncertain of herself. She was a paralegal with tons of confidence at her job. This? This was new territory.

As they prepared to land, Cat wiped her clammy hands down the sides of her sundress. She could do this.

She'd go straight to the hotel, have a bite, and collapse in bed. It was late, and she had zero plans the next day on purpose.

The bellhop took her bags from the taxi's trunk, and Cat paid the cab driver. She walked through the revolving door and took in her surroundings.

The hotel was everything she'd dreamed of—open, breezy, well-appointed without being over the top. Low, deep sofas and chairs scattered on an oversized tile floor that stretched out to the pool area. Dim light filled the back gardens and outlined the vast infinity pool. In the dark of night, she couldn't see the ocean, but the salty smell lingered.

"Good evening. Welcome to the resort." The front desk receptionist had smooth cocoa skin and wore a fuchsia skirt suit. She greeted Cat with a warm smile.

"Hello. I'm Catherine Dalton. Checking in."

"Yes, Miss Dalton." She clicked on her keyboard, verified Cat's I.D., and handed her a key. "You are in suite five-forty. The resort is all-inclusive," she slid a brochure over the counter, "so here are the services and amenities that are included in your package. If you would like to go to town, simply schedule with the valets ahead of time. Please enjoy your stay, and don't hesitate to ask if there is anything you need."

Cat returned the smile, simply thankful to not get called Mrs. Sumners. She owed that to Celeste and the girls.

The bellhop escorted her to her room, and after a brief introduction of where things were, she tipped him before he left.

Wow! The suite was beautiful. A luxurious oversized bed with crisp white linens, a large pale blue and salmon

Oriental rug over marble tile flooring, and soft linen drapes that flowed gently at an open sliding glass door leading to the balcony.

"Jack, you have outdone yourself." She appreciated the hotel, her room, but mostly she was glad to have landed and was only minutes from a comfy bed.

If she didn't cry herself to sleep, that would be a bonus.

The next morning, sun spilled through the windows, touches of gilded gold on everything. Cat had tossed and turned before finally settling into a deep coma of sleep. She glanced at the time. Ten a.m.

She must have needed—she did the math in her head—eleven hours of sleep.

Geez!

She reached for her phone and shot off a text to Celeste, who immediately replied.

So glad you made it! Have fun. Drink drinks with umbrellas and fruit. Get a massage and facial. Create the next Cat Dalton work of art. Cel xx

Cat chuckled out loud. It felt good to laugh, even if it was only briefly.

She flung her suitcase on the king-sized bed and proceeded to unpack her clothes. Under her jeans she noticed the sexy pink lingerie—Cel must have snuck it in her bag. She lifted the bra, running her fingertips over the lace.

Cat gasped. Beneath the lingerie was a box with the image of a pink vibrator. Holy cow!

She opened the box and brought the item closer for inspection. Cat had a vibrator at home, somewhere. But it wasn't nearly as big as this, and not so life-like. This was thick and had bumpy lines and ridges like a real man would have. Heat rose in her cheeks just holding the implement.

Knowing Cel, it was probably already charged. *Clearly she thought this would be encouraging—stretching my boundaries and all that.*

Cat stuck the box in the nightstand drawer—sex was the last thing on her mind—and finished unpacking.

After putting her clothes away, she slipped on her bathing suit, cover-up and hat, grabbed the hotel brochure, and headed to the pool. She sat at a small table off to the side and ordered the largest egg breakfast they offered.

She was famished, and it didn't bother her in the least when the waiter's eyes went big at her breakfast selection.

Now to fill some of this time so I don't spend it thinking about that asshole, she thought.

She flipped open the brochure and read the highlights:

Seven restaurants and shops, including a nightclub
Full spa and salon with massage, facial, nails, hair, makeup

Gym and sauna

Daily snorkeling and paddle boarding

Movie theater

Live bands

Two pools and a hot tub

Concierge services

Local area transportation

Her itinerary included several spa services during the two-week respite. She should be doing backflips but instead she just felt sorta numb. Glancing around the resort at the happy couples, she decided screw it. This was her vacation.

One day at a time.

After breakfast, she lifted her mimosa and walked out to the beach. The soft, warm sand crunched under her feet and squished between her toes. Salty air filled her nostrils. The clear blue water stretched to the horizon, the waves creating a soothing lull. She found a lounge chair under a cabana and propped up her legs.

Cat took several deeps breaths of fresh ocean air and decided she needed a plan. But that idea sailed out into the ocean as she closed her eyes "for just a minute" and woke up two hours later.

She stretched, reaching her hands past the lounger, and laughed. She could *not* come all the way to this fabulous island and sleep the entire time. Oh, the ribbing she would get from Celeste would be never-ending.

She hoisted herself off the lounger and went to the concierge desk to plan an agenda. Not every waking moment, but a little something each day. Something to look forward to.

"I would also like to take a trip or two off the resort to do some sketching," she told the young man dressed in black and white.

"Yes, Miss. We can arrange for that. Any place in particular?"

What did she want? "I don't exactly know, but maybe some old buildings, churches, or bridges." She shrugged her shoulder.

The concierge glanced at the brochures beside the desk. "I will make a list of recommendations and leave it at the front desk for you to retrieve tonight. Then you can just select what you want and the driver will take you there."

What more could she ask for? "Thanks."

She stepped onto the elevator, barely aware of the man who followed. She thought of the concierge's suggestion of a list and wondered what to choose first. Maybe there would be an old courthouse or a church at Anse La Raye she could draw.

"Must be a really good thought."

His voice pulled her out of her daydream and she observed the man beside her in dress slacks and a knit collared shirt with an emblem over the chest. His smile seemed genuine, and she realized she must have been smiling too.

"I guess it was."

"That's how vacations are supposed to be, right?" His blue eyes shone and he gripped the handle of his suitcase, then wheeled it off the elevator. "Have a good stay," he said before the doors closed.

That was nice, she thought. Nice-looking guy too.

Cat startled as the elevator descended and quickly pushed the number five. She'd been so distracted that she'd forgotten to press the button when she'd first gotten on.

Having a plan would allow her some control over this strange situation. Maybe she'd actually enjoy herself for two weeks. Indulge in some R&R, try out some new things, go exploring. As long as she didn't think about Jack specifically, she knew she'd be alright.

CHAPTER
Four

Cat decided starting a vacation with a massage was the right way to go. She lucked out when she called the spa Tuesday morning and they had an opening.

The previous night, she'd picked up the concierge's recommendations of places to visit and then updated her two-week agenda. She looked forward to something for once that didn't revolve around the wedding. She'd caught a glimpse of the vibe Celeste had packed for her and chuckled. Some things might stay off the agenda.

After a late breakfast, she entered the hotel's posh spa five minutes early. Soft, instrumental music played in the background and the scent of vanilla filled the air. "Hello. I have an appointment at eleven for a massage."

"Excellent. You would be Miss Dalton?"

"That's correct."

"Can I get you a glass of fruit-infused cold water before I take you back to Sebastian?"

What? Her back straightened. A male masseur? The

idea hadn't even occurred to Cat. Of course, it was possible, and not that it really mattered, but... Well, she couldn't say why she was apprehensive.

"Is everything alright, Miss Dalton?"

Calm down, Cat. You have nothing to worry about. Just because she'd never had a male massage therapist before didn't mean there was anything to be wary of. Jack might have been the last man to touch her, but Cat couldn't expect for that to last forever. Eventually there would be men...

"Everything is great. And yes, I'd love some water." She chased away the apprehension and forced a casual smile.

She followed the receptionist back to a cozy, softly lit room. "Make yourself comfortable. I'll be right back with your water."

True to her word, the receptionist returned shortly with a glass of ice water. "Sebastian will be with you in a few moments. Enjoy." The young woman pivoted on her heel and left, closing the door behind her.

Cat sank into the upholstered bench and sipped her water. A male. Cat'd never had a massage given by a man before. Only ever a woman. She shook her head. She was overreacting. Not to mention, if he was gay, he'd have no interest in her.

The door opened quietly, pulling her from her thoughts. A tall, dark-haired, brown-eyed man walked into the massage room and smiled at her. His white, short-sleeve uniform shirt pulled snuggly over his shoulders and chest muscles. His waist was trim and his skin bronzed.

My! He was a fine specimen of a man.

"Miss Dalton, I'm Sebastian. I'll perform your massage today." He had an exotic Latin American accent. He leaned forward, offering his hand.

She hesitantly reached for it, allowing his large warm hand to engulf hers. "Hello."

His brow furrowed softly. "I apologize for being late. My previous appointment was delayed. If you could remove your clothes and jewelry, and lie face-up on the massage table, I'll return in a few moments, and we'll get started."

She swallowed hard. He certainly didn't *act* gay. "Sure," she choked out.

Sebastian left the room. Her heart beat faster. She could do this. Not all men were untrustworthy slime balls.

Cat stripped, hiding her underthings beneath her cotton tee and shorts. She gulped some cool water and climbed onto the table, under the covers. The table seemed wider than a traditional massage table. Not that that would matter for a tall man like Sebastian.

She pulled up the sheet, letting the soft cotton envelope her, brushing lightly against her bare form.

A soft knock at the door announced his return. Cat's eyes were squeezed shut; she forced her face to relax.

"Comfortable?" She heard him adjust the music, then the lamp to darken the room, before he gathered his lotion.

"Yes."

"Any areas that feel particularly tight, Miss Dalton?"

She opened her eyes to see him looking down at her. Oh, she'd better not regret this.

"Cat, please. No. I just need to relax," her tone sounded curt. *Shoot!* Why had she said that? Keep it together, she scolded herself.

"I can see that. Well, take a few deep breaths for me. I will start with your head and work my way to your toes. Then you will turn over and I'll repeat the same process on the backside. If anything feels tight, and needs more work, please let me know. Also, if something is uncomfortable, let me know so I can stop. All right?"

Sebastian may look straight off the Man of the Year calendar, but he was professional and attentive, and Cat appreciated that.

"Yes. Thank you."

She closed her eyes again when Sebastian's fingers smoothed her hair off her face in light, feathery strokes. He applied an oil to his fingers and started massaging her face and neck, going into her hairline.

Quietly, he said, "I can see you have a lot on your mind. Try and calm your thoughts. Be here in the moment. Find peace."

He'd hit the nail on the head. She had a lot on her mind—cheating fiancés that lied through their teeth, and now, literally putting herself in another man's hands.

43

She forced a deeper breath. She could do this. She *needed* a massage. Sebastian was a professional. She wanted to kick her vacation off with a bang. And she deserved it, dammit!

His hands moved over her neck and shoulders, making a few passes between her breasts. She was sure it wasn't intended to be a sexual thing, but it certainly felt sensual. His hands were warm and the pace of his movements helped her nerves and muscles start to calm.

Finishing her arms, he moved the blanket aside to pull her right leg out. Applying more oil, he worked his strong hands up and down. His thumbs pressed firmly into her quads and a tiny moan passed her lips.

Heat rose in her cheeks. She'd never moaned with a female masseuse.

Cat tensed slightly when his hands worked their way upward, very close to her sex. She swallowed. His fingers never touched her *there*, instead they merely grazed passed to work her right hip and a bit of her stomach. Dang! Her muscles were tight. After several minutes, he covered the right leg and repeated the procedure on her left leg.

She noticed the blanket wasn't really tucked in anywhere. In fact, moisture had begun to gather at the apex of her thighs, and whenever the blanket shifted, air sent a coolness over her vulva.

Her heartbeat increased slightly, but a hypnotic state also settled in. She felt so incredibly relaxed that she didn't bother opening her eyes or care if any private parts were exposed. Sebastian had magic fingers. Her earlier nervousness was for no good reason.

He re-covered her leg and whispered, "Please turn over, Cat."

He held the blanket to conceal her breasts. She rotated and placed her face in the padded face rest. She inhaled and a sweet scent of vanilla filled her senses. Sebastian lowered the sheet to her waist, maybe past her waist. She couldn't be sure, but some of her derriere might be exposed. Her muscles tensed.

He whispered close to her ear, "Relax. Relaxation is good for your blood pressure, your memory, so many things."

Right. She tried to calm down and focus on not letting her anxiety ruin her wonderful massage.

His oiled hands began long strokes up and down her back. He kneaded and worked out knots along the way. She breathed deeply. *Oh yeah.*

The sensual feeling flowing through her, coupled with the deep relaxation, brought Cat to a place she had rarely been. Simply euphoric. Sebastian massaged her arms, leaving them limp and pliable. He covered her torso and moved to her left leg next, this time exposing half her ass. However, when his hands began to stroke her leg, hip, and butt cheek in deep, satisfying, rhythmic glides, she didn't have the energy to give it much thought.

An achiness built as Sebastian's motions continued. He moved to the right leg. Again her right ass cheek was bared to him, to the room, to his marvelous hands.

A moan slipped passed her lips, and she wished she could reach down to take care of the blossoming need at her sex. Maybe she would have a use for the vibe after all.

After several minutes, he re-covered her leg, and she feared the massage was over. That was sixty minutes? Damn! But it was so good. Worth every blessed penny! Every one of Jack's pennies!

She felt his breath at her ear, and his hand at her lip. "Lift your hips and I will slide a pillow underneath."

Confused, she met his gaze. "My massage isn't over?"

He shook his head. "You don't have to be finished. If you'll let me, I can help you. Help you to completely relax." He spoke the words in a most professional manner, but his deep chocolate eyes told a different story. "Would you like my help, Cat?"

Holy crap! Was he offering what she thought he was offering? Her heart pounded against her ribcage. What should she do? She couldn't allow this. No. But wouldn't a release be welcome right now? NO.

Ugh. She somehow knew she could trust him. Trust that he could take care of her need and yet expect nothing more.

And she had to admit, any amount of trust in a man right now was huge.

But was she crazy to do this? This was off the charts of adventurous, right?

Double holy crap!

She licked her lips and, taking a chance, she nodded.

She raised her hips off the table slightly. He slid his forearm under her, along her belly, and lifted her the rest of the way. With his other hand, he slipped a fluffy pillow under her hips.

She could only imagine what she looked like with her ass protruding off the table.

His hands returned to her ankles and feet. She remained covered as he slid underneath the blanket to massage her legs in long strokes. With each pass, he went higher, at the same time, he spread her legs a little farther apart. Up and down he went. His warm hands finally made it to her ass cheeks—one on each globe.

The blanket collected on her thighs. He made another pass—down to her ankles and slid back up to her ass. More blanket bunched at her hips. A cool breeze of air over her exposed sex sent a shiver through her.

Oh my. Another rush of moisture filled her sex. This had to be the most erotic thing she'd ever experienced. Her heart pounded.

Another pass over her legs and this time the blanket rested at her low back, completely exposing her sex and ass to him.

She lay on this table with her ass raised up, legs spread,

and his fingers working the tiny muscles at the top of her thighs. Finally, one strong finger glossed through her slit, spreading her moisture around.

"Oh," she breathed.

He so gently stroked her slit with his fingers, making brief passes over her clit and bringing the whole area alive. She heard him shift, even as his fingers stayed in place. His voice was at her ear. "May I use my tongue?"

Oh, mercy. His fingers never stopped moving. Thinking became difficult. If this man was as talented with his tongue as he was with his fingers, she would die and go to heaven.

She replayed her new mantra: *Be adventurous.* She took in air. "Yes," she whispered.

He maneuvered to the end of the table again, and his fingers gently spread her apart. In a beat, his tongue was on her clit. She moaned aloud.

Glorious. In no time, he would have her coming. His tongue massaged over her clit and through her core, poking inside and swirling around.

Her breath escalated to panting.

His strong hands spread her farther apart, but not to the point of pain. His tongue never stopped the delicious torture.

"Sebastian," she breathed.

He didn't let up, and she knew she was closing in on something spectacular. Leveraging her arms, she lifted her ass even more. He groaned.

He applied more pressure with his tongue, and God help her, she didn't want it to end. This had to be the best oral sex she'd ever received.

As if sensing her desires, Sebastian left her clit and continued his licks in areas nearby: soft parts of skin, her smooth ass cheeks, and over her lips.

He returned to her clit more gently this time. He teased her, and Cat's clit swelled, longing for friction. Longing for release.

Without notice, the slow creep of her orgasm began, sending a warmth throughout her body. Building and building, she finally exploded, muffling her scream into the headrest. She was fairly sure she squirted on Sebastian's tongue.

Slowly, her muscles relaxed, and her hips lowered back onto the pillow.

Sebastian carefully covered her body and slipped the pillow out from under her hips. His hands traveled several times over the sheet on her back.

"Take as much time as you need. This room is vacant for another hour." He leaned closer. "Cat, look at me."

Did she have to? She was a little freaked. Mortified, really. She raised her head to find Sebastian's mere inches away.

"You are exquisite," he said in a low tone. "You are beautiful inside and out. Don't ever believe otherwise." He lifted the back of her hand to his lips for a gentle kiss. "You are absolutely beautiful when you come. You will make some man incredibly, insanely happy." His smile was sweet and genuine. He kissed her hand one last time before he straightened to leave.

Whoa! What was that? The most incredible orgasm, given to her by an exotic, sexy stranger, and it felt positively euphoric. Out of this world. She exhaled. This would be a day Cat would not soon forget.

In a strange way, she felt powerful, and her self-confidence rose. What if the compliments from Sebastian were real? Not some flowery crap to make her feel good because he wanted a big tip.

Her whole body hummed with the after-glow of her orgasm, but it was more than that. The way he'd moved over her naked body made her feel beautiful. The way she'd come so easily? Empowered.

She sat up, leaving the blanket on the table. She felt new.

That was pretty adventurous, huh?

She chuckled quietly—taking a chance had paid off.

Her story wasn't yet written. She got to decide the end. She could decide what would happen next. She wouldn't let Jackass Jack determine her future or her worth.

She didn't need Sebastian and his marvelous gift to figure all of this out. She would have gotten there in her own time, eventually. She reached for her shorts. Sooner was better than later.

CHAPTER
Five

Cat spied a small resting alcove off to the side, with a perfect view of the ocean and far enough away from the pool to have some quiet where she could enjoy her after-massage glow.

With her sketchpad in hand, she approached the poolside bartender. "I'd like a fruit smoothie?"

"Absolutely, miss," he replied with a smile.

"Great, can you deliver it over there?" She pointed across the ginormous pool to the cozy area partitioned by shrubbery.

"The Palm Patio. Yes, miss."

She meandered along the concrete path. "The Palm Patio," she whispered. "I like it."

She chose a wrought iron table and sank down into the chair, smiling at the only other couple. They were so caught up in each other they hardly noticed her.

No doubt newlyweds, Cat thought.

With a sigh, she opened her sketchbook and reminded

herself not to think about cheating assholes and jilted brides-to-be.

The bartender delivered her fruit smoothie and confirmed her room number.

She forgot to say "no straw", but next time. She sipped. *Wow!* The mango and peach awakened her taste buds. She took another sip. After her incredible morning, she didn't want a heavy lunch. Sweet, cool, and refreshing. This hit the spot.

Staring at the blank page, her mind wandered freely. What did she want to sketch? She pulled a medium charcoal from her box and began with some simple lines—straight and curved.

She tilted her head to the side. She added some short strokes, layering them horizontally. Smudging lightly for effect. Her palm tree was taking shape. Maybe she'd add another one so it wasn't lonely.

The lines came slowly. She was a little rusty, having spent zero time on her craft in the last year. But it felt good just the same. She barely noticed someone hovering close until a shadow covered half her pad.

She stopped and lifted her head. The person who stood beside her was the same man she'd seen in the elevator the day before.

"I'm sorry to bother you. That's very good." He spoke with no detectable island accent. He smiled, and his gaze traveled from her sketch to her eyes.

"Thanks."

He shifted his water glass to his left hand and offered his right. "Nicholas Westbrook."

She wiped her hand on her napkin and shook his. "Catherine Dalton."

"Nice to meet you, Catherine." He nudged his chin toward her sketchbook. "Is this a job or a hobby?"

He slipped off his sunglasses. His blue eyes twinkled in the afternoon sunlight, their hue as rich as the ocean before her. His dark brown hair had a shine that any woman would envy.

"Please call me Cat. And this is more hobby than anything."

He took a seat at the table next to hers. "Well, you're very talented."

The corners of her lips pulled upward. She hadn't had a compliment on her art in a long time. She missed it. "Thank you."

"What do you do when you're not creating art?"

"I'm a paralegal. What do you do?"

"I work for a wine and liquor distributor—this is my sales territory. I like to stay at this resort and branch out from here. Over the next three weeks, I'll cover several of the Caribbean Islands."

That explains the logo shirts.

A waitress arrived carrying what looked like a jerk chicken salad and placed it before him. "Can I get you anything else, sir?"

"No. This is great." He turned toward Cat. "What brings you to Saint Lucia?"

Shit! She hadn't planned for this. She hadn't expected to have to answer these kinds of questions. She swallowed hard. "It was supposed to be my honeymoon."

He paused. "I'm so sorry."

"It's okay. I mean, best to learn now than later."

Nicholas narrowed his eyes. "You caught him cheating?"

"Yup."

"Damn." He shook his head back and forth several times.

They sat in silence for a while. She sketched while he ate. When he was finished, he asked. "How'd you like to have dinner with me tonight?"

"Oh, I don't think—"

"You gotta eat, right? So do I. We could just eat together." The sheepish grin that crossed his face was pretty adorable, Cat had to admit.

This wasn't what this trip was about. *It's just dinner.* She lifted a shoulder. "Okay." *Why not? The company might be nice.*

"Great. How about we meet at the Seaside restaurant at seven. That will give me time to visit a few more clients on the island, and you time for sketching," he said with a smile.

"I'll meet you there."

He dropped his napkin on the table and rose to offer his hand. "Nice to meet you, Cat Dalton. I'll see you in a few hours."

"See you soon."

She watched him leave and couldn't help but notice what a nice backside he had. She wasn't in the market for a man. God, no. But if she was going to be alone for two weeks, an occasional someone to talk to might be good.

As she returned to her sketch, she thought, it's just dinner.

"So where are you from?" Nicholas asked as the waiter refilled their wine glasses.

"Austin. Lived there all my life. What about you?" She scooped up some rice pilaf and chewed. Everything tasted exquisite, so fresh. The smoothie at lunch hadn't stayed with her long enough.

"Orlando. I actually moved there for this job five years ago. They wanted someone close to cover the islands."

"So you go around from resort to resort?"

He sipped his chardonnay. "Yup. Resorts, hotels, and several restaurants and bars."

"Wow. Cool job."

He gave her a nod. "It can be. Of course, it creates a challenge when trying to sustain a relationship."

"Ah, yes. The traveling salesman." She dabbed the

corner of her mouth with her cloth napkin and returned it to her lap.

Swallowing his bite of shrimp, he blotted his lips and met her gaze. "Mind if I ask what happened? With the ex."

"No. Not much to tell." She tipped her head, debating how much crap she wanted to off-load on unsuspecting Nicholas. "We'd been dating for just about two years. I caught him with some blonde two days before we were supposed to get married."

"Ouch. What an asshole." His face scrunched up like he'd swallowed a cockroach.

"He said I wasn't adventurous enough. Not a risk taker."

"I'm sorry that happened to you."

"Thanks," she replied nonchalantly, trying to keep some emotional distance from the whole incident. Not to mention, any sort of breakdown at the restaurant would likely be frowned upon.

"So he was trying to cram in as much fun as he could before getting hitched."

She took a long drink from her glass and pointed straight at him. "Bingo."

He nodded slowly, thoughtfully. "I actually think most times men bring that out of their women. Or visa-versa. It's something they share together. But if the woman trusts the man, she's more willing to try new things. If the trust isn't there, it makes it harder to step out of your comfort zone. In my opinion."

She'd never thought of it that way. Nicholas wasn't trying to make any assumptions about her and Jack. In fact, he just might have a point, but regardless, she would take some time before she even needed to question trusting a guy in a relationship again. She'd *thought* she could trust Jack... Anyway, relationships were going on the back burner for a while.

The conversation flowed through the rest of dinner effortlessly. Cat pushed back in her chair, relaxed, sipping her wine as the waiter cleared their plates.

An odd sort of peace and realization came over her. Anytime she'd gone to dinner with Jack, she sat straight and always looked attentive or interested in anything he had to say. Had she been trying too hard and not really being herself?

Nah. That wasn't possible. It wasn't like she'd been uncomfortable sitting forward in her chair to listen to him. Still, there may have been a few times she'd wanted to roll her eyes as Jack told his football stories or his near-death skydiving tale yet again. But didn't all couples go through that? Eventually one knew all their partner's stories, right?

"Would you like some dessert, Cat?"

"No thanks. I'm stuffed. The sea bass was incredible."

"Good. I'm glad you liked it." He motioned the waiter for the check. Although everything was included in their stay at the resort, they were still expected to sign the bill. "Would you like to work off some of the dinner with a walk along the beach?"

That sounded suspiciously like a date, but she was only here for another eleven days, so what harm could it cause? Nothing monumental could happen in such a small about of time.

"Sure. Sounds nice."

They walked out to the patio, past the pool, to the edge of the sandy beach.

"Want to take off your sandals?" He sat on the lounger and slipped off his shoes.

She did, and hooked the straps of her shoes over her fingers.

They strolled along the beach, mostly empty of tourists. The sun would set in about thirty minutes.

He gently steered her to the right, letting his hand linger on her waist.

An inexplicable shiver raced down her spine.

His hand dropped as they casually walked side by side. "So have you done much since you arrived?"

She dipped her head to hide the blush she felt rush to her cheeks. Celeste might not even hear about her spontaneous and surprising massage. "Um, not really. Just arrived Sunday."

"Well, there's a great flea market, if you like that kind of thing. Plus water and rainforest excursions."

She looked over at him. The dusky light shined in his

eyes making the hue a stunning sapphire blue, drawing her in and making it hard to turn away.

"Did I say something wrong?"

Heat rose in her cheeks again. "No. Sorry." She faced straight ahead. "I actually made an itinerary of sorts. And the concierge recommended some cool buildings I might want to draw."

"Excellent."

"Yup. Tomorrow I plan to have a driver take me downtown to an old courthouse."

Nicholas nodded, and they continued their stroll, passing hotels and resorts, office buildings, and a few people lounging on towels or chairs. He asked a few more questions about her art and when she'd learned to draw.

They stopped as the sun dipped low in the horizon, creating a beautiful kaleidoscope of ambers and orange-reds against a deep-blue sky.

"This is one of the coolest things about my job," he mused.

She smiled. "No doubt. Mother Nature at its finest."

Nicholas turned to face her. "Cat, I can't imagine what you must be going through. I mean, if something like that happened to me just before I was supposed to get married, I would be brimming with anger and hurt." He inhaled. "I don't know why you decided to go on your honeymoon anyway, but I'm really glad you did. I don't want to crowd you, but would you like to have dinner with me the day after tomorrow? Tomorrow night, I'll be in Antigua."

Did she want to go down that road? She wasn't here for romance. She'd come to get away from hurt, anger, embarrassment, and frankly to rethink some key beliefs in her life that just may be holding her back in the future. Holding her back from being her best self.

She nibbled on her lip. Would sharing dinner with Nicholas really prevent her from accomplishing her goals?

She gazed out at the ocean. "Why not?"

He grinned. "Perfect."

They strolled on, enjoying the melodic sounds of the gentle waves washing in and out. They talked more about his work and hers, a little bit about some movies they'd each seen, and what they were looking forward to. Although he had family all over the country, most of her family was in Texas.

Before she knew it, they'd walked for a mile or so, circled back, and night had settled in. She tipped her head. The stars above sparkled like they'd been waiting all day to shine their brilliance for everyone to see.

He stopped her in front of their resort, the beach bare of people. "Cat, would it be alright if I kissed you goodnight?"

Okay, this is definitely turning into more than just dinner.

Again, what could happen in her short stay on the island? And honestly, she wondered what his kisses would be like. "Yes."

He stepped closer and glazed the back of his fingers up her neck, over her jaw, to her cheeks. He cupped her face as he lowered his mouth to hers. His firm lips placed small pecks, then he nibbled a bit. Her lips parted slightly, and he tested, his warm tongue reaching for hers.

He closed the gap, leaving no air between them. She clasped her hands around his shoulders, allowing his warmth to penetrate her. This was her first "first kiss" in so long. She hadn't expected to have this again, but it felt so damn good.

He dipped into her mouth deeper. He tasted of wine and hot male.

Her tongue tangled with his, craving more, learning a new dance with one another.

Finally, he broke the kiss. They panted lightly, and he stared straight into her eyes. His gaze mirrored what she wanted—more.

"Wow," he breathed. "Thank you."

She chuckled, her cheeks hot from the intensity. "You're welcome."

He walked her to her room, his fingers intertwined with hers. When they arrived, he gave her one last kiss, less passionate than the one on the beach. "Two days will feel like two years." He waited for her to open her door.

She smiled and waved, and watched him walk down the hall toward the elevators. The door closed behind her; she bolted it and leaned against it for the stability.

That kiss. She might never forget that incredible kiss. She giggled. What would Celeste say?

CHAPTER
Six

Nicholas landed at Antigua International Airport with only one thing on his mind—Cat.

He shuffled through the lines at baggage claim and customs. Some of the airport employees recognized him from his years of visiting the island. Sometimes when he travelled, one day melted into the next. There was no real variety to his job, but it paid *very* well, so he didn't want to give it up. What's more, once he got his promotion to Regional Manager—probably in a year or two—most of this monotonous travel would cease.

Success was what drove Nic. Really the whole family. His sister had an Intellectual Property law practice in Charlotte. His brother was a cardiac surgeon in Atlanta. Nic might not be as successful as his siblings, in terms of prestige or money, but one day he would top them both. Until then, the only relationships for Nic were the casual kind.

This trip—after meeting Cat—things seemed a little brighter. The vast ocean was bluer and the sky clearer. For the first time, he'd stopped and smelled the bouquet of flowers in the resort's lobby that morning on his way to the airport.

He chuckled as he hauled his luggage into the trunk of the rental car. Cat was definitely a sexy distraction. In the five years of traveling for his job, he'd maybe gone to bed with a woman a handful of times. They'd known it was a passing fling and meant nothing beyond two people enjoying each other's company.

Being with Cat didn't have that same casual feel. No. In this case, he'd need to tread lightly. He was drawn to her in an inexplicable way, but she was coming off an insane break-up. Devastated, she was understandably cautious, and he'd respect that. By the same token, he wanted to see her again. Had to see her again.

Nic had ten stops planned for the day. In the morning, he had appointments with buyers and general managers of resorts and hotels. Later he'd meet with bar and restaurant contacts. He only had a few new wine varieties and one flavored vodka to talk about. Nevertheless, it was always good to get facetime with folks and make sure they were happy with their level of service.

Every once in a while, Nicholas was thrown a curve ball. A shipment was wrong or late, and he'd hear all about it. He'd learned quickly not to take it personally, and do his damnedest to fix the problem. He hadn't lost a client yet. That might be another reason the company paid him so well.

And promised him a Regional Manager position.

After a handful of successful morning meetings, he arrived at his next appointment just before lunch—Sandos Antigua Resort. Raquel Domingues greeted him immediately. She was part-owner of this posh resort with her husband Rocky. They'd been long-time customers, and over the years Nic had learned Raquel was a huge flirt.

"Nicholas, darling, you made it." She approached him in a snug, short black skirt and a pale-blue silk button-down blouse. The length of her necklace dipped down into her cleavage. Her sun-kissed skin made her look vivacious and sexy. No doubt about it.

Nic leaned forward, allowing her to kiss each cheek, while scanning the lobby for signs of Rocky. "Good morning, Raquel."

"Come. Let's go to my office and chat."

He followed her, asking, "Will Rocky be joining us?"

She glanced back and grinned. "No. Does that bother you? He's meeting with the landscaper about a retaining wall on the east side."

He grinned back. "No problem at all." She was essentially harmless. All flirt, no action. But most importantly, married women were off-limits.

She motioned to a chair—two were situated in front of her large wooden desk—and closed the door behind her.

"So, you look well. Have you been working out?" She stroked his upper arm.

He smiled, unconcerned by her touch. It was an inoffensive gesture, one she'd used several times before. "I do what I can."

"Good for you. It's hard sometimes, making time for the gym when work demands your attention twenty-four-seven."

"Raquel, you're doing great. Whatever you're doing keep it up." It wasn't shallow flattery. The woman loved to hear compliments and was likely fishing for one. Nic would need to be careful that she didn't read too much into it.

She smiled broadly before pushing paper and knick-knacks out of the way on her desk, leaving him room to display his liquor bottles.

"So what yumminess do you have for me today?"

One at a time, he opened the wines, pouring samples, and discussing the nuances and pairings of each. Raquel savored the wine as it was a favorite of hers.

"These are delicious. I especially like the cabernet, maybe with a steak or beef entrée."

He nodded.

"I'll take several cases."

"Great. Lastly, I have an orange-cranberry vodka that's getting lots of rave reviews."

He lifted the bottle from his case and she stopped it, raising her hand. "Hang on. Have you had lunch?"

Nic made it a policy to eat, whenever possible, at his customers' establishments. He thought it was only right to reciprocate the business. "Not yet."

"Let's go to the bar. I actually want Julian to try it."

He nodded and stood to pack his bottles. Nic wasn't surprised by her request. Julian was the head bartender and would weigh in on buying decisions frequently.

Raquel looped her arm through Nic's and led him toward the front of the building where the bar was open for lunch and dinner. The space had an understated opulence meant to cater to the well-off clientele at Sandos. It had a long Cuban Mahogany bar with a gleaming Lucite counter, clothed tables topped with votive candles, and windows with shutters only cracked open an inch or two. Unlike the rest of the décor in the resort—light, airy, and colorful—the bar had a dark, sophisticated polish that made you want to relax with a glass of whiskey and savor life for a while.

Raquel leaned against the bar, waving at Julian.

"Hi Raquel. Nicholas, how've you been?" Julian offered his hand.

"Great, Julian. Good to see you."

"Nico—" Raquel started.

This was the first time she'd used a nickname for him. He ducked his head and opened his case to hide his surprise. The tiny hairs on the back of his neck curled.

"Has a new vodka he wants us to try."

"Excellent." Julian reached beneath the counter and retrieved three shot glasses.

Nic poured, then set the bottle in front of Julian to

peruse. They toasted and sipped.

"Strong." Julian nodded. "Powerful polish."

"I agree," Raquel chimed in. "Tastes expensive."

Nic turned the price list in their direction.

Raquel lifted her perfectly shaped brow. "What do you think, Julian?"

"I say we give it a try. I'll play with it and see what specialty cocktail I can mix up."

"Super." She faced Nic. "Put us down for a case." Her hand went to his upper arm. "Now, how about some lunch?"

Julian handed her two menus.

Nic lifted his case and followed her to an empty table in the back corner.

"What would you like to drink?" she asked, situating her blouse collar.

"Iced tea, please."

The waitress greeted them.

"An iced tea for our guest, and a white wine spritzer for me. Julian knows how I like it."

"Very well, ma'am." The waitress smiled and pivoted toward the bar.

They quietly scanned the menu. He still had a full day and opted for a salad so he wouldn't feel weighed down.

"You look well. How've you been?" Raquel asked, relaxing into her chair.

"Thanks. I've been busy. I'll visit about twelve islands in the Lesser Antilles this trip."

"Wow. Good for you. I hope your company appreciates you. You are a definite asset."

He smiled, not entirely sure what to make of her comment.

After they ordered, he asked, "How are things going for you? I like the new sign."

Her eyes twinkled. "Yeah, finally got Rocky to agree to the expense. I helped design it, and I love the finished product."

"Looks good."

"Otherwise, nothing new to report. Same ol' same ol'." She sipped her wine. "I was actually looking forward to your visit."

His senses went on high-alert. Before he had an opportunity to ask what she meant, the waitress set down their entrees.

"Thanks, Lucy."

He took a long drink of tea, wetting his suddenly dry throat. He hoped he wasn't misinterpreting the signals Raquel was putting out.

She leaned closer to him, laying her hand on his thigh.

He nearly jumped, and regrettably something stirred to life.

She met his gaze straight on and lowered her voice. "Nico, I was hoping you might have a few extra minutes for your long-time customer." The corners of her lips curved as she stroked his thigh under the tablecloth.

His groin tightened on its own accord.

He'd held off advances from women before and, as attractive as Raquel kept herself, he might have entertained her offer. If the circumstances were different, like if she were single.

He rested his hand over hers, stopping her progress. "Raquel, you know I adore you, and I have an affinity for brilliant businesswomen," he said with a wink, "but there's *no* chance of that happening." He kept eye contact, hoping that ended the conversation and nothing more needed to be discussed. And hoping to high heaven that didn't just cost him the account.

Raquel pulled back her hand and cleared her throat. "Absolutely. Thank you for the compliment." She sent him a genuine smile. "I know how much you care about Rocky too."

"I do."

"Very good. Let's dig in. It looks delicious." She pointed to his salad. "I ventured out today and got the salmon. Chef said he wanted to try some new recipes for the summer season."

And that was that. She took his rejection like a pro. Nic admired the hell out of her. Truly. But the one woman he wanted stroking his thigh—or any part of his body—was two-hundred and twenty miles away. Probably lounging in a hammock, sketching something new, and sipping on a drink with an umbrella stuck in it.

He shoveled a bite in to hide his smile.

Cat was a breath of fresh air. Her quiet, restrained disposition mixed with the right amount of friendly optimism had him captivated.

Later that evening, Nic collapsed on his bed. He was spent. He didn't even think he had the energy to order room service for dinner.

In fact, there was only one thing he wanted to do—talk to Cat.

Cat finished her nighttime routine and was about to open an ebook when a text came through. *Nicholas.*

Hi stranger. You still awake?

She couldn't say why she was so excited to receive his text. Was this what people meant when they talked about a "rebound guy"? Because, really, shouldn't she be mourning the loss of a relationship?

Hi! Yes. Getting ready for bed. Have a good day?

She walked to the dresser and pulled out her boxers and cami.

Yes. Good day, but a busy one. I wish I was there to kiss you goodnight.

She reread the message because she wasn't sure she'd read it right. Wow! She didn't know how to reply.

His next text hit her phone in a beat.

I'm sorry. I didn't mean to overstep.

God, she was so confused. She loved his comment. She

would love it if he were there, kissing her goodnight. But how was that possible? Less than a week prior she'd caught her fiancé screwing another woman. She wanted to be honest with Nicholas.

You didn't. I like that thought. Just surprised myself, I guess.

Surprised because it wasn't so long ago that you broke off your engagement?

Yes.

There was a pause of several moments and she wondered if they'd somehow lost their cellular connection. She crawled in between the covers and finally he responded.

Cat, I'm drawn to you. I'm sorry that I'm not doing a good job of hiding it. Because I don't want to put any pressure on you.

She thought about that for a minute. Again she wanted to be honest; she just didn't know how much was built on the heels of rebound and how much were true feelings.

She swallowed hard.

Please don't hide anything from me. I'm drawn to you too.

God, Cat. I can't wait to get back there. I can't wait for dinner. I have a big day

tomorrow. I'm gonna head to bed. I'll
probably dream of you. Good night.

☺ *Night!*

She would probably dream of him too. Her face had already grown warm. She felt a dull ache deep inside and wondered if it would go away. *Not likely.*

She imagined Nicholas at her door, perhaps after dinner, his hand cupping the back of her neck to lean down and kiss her. A deep kiss, an all-encompassing kiss. She could picture his ocean-blue eyes staring into hers, silently asking if he could have more. Asking if he could claim her, even if just for the short time she was on the island.

If he wanted more, she might give him more. Geez! Was that crazy? Having a fling with a stranger, sex with a man she'd only just met, so soon after breaking off her engagement.

Her hands roamed over her belly subconsciously. She needed to quell this ache. Celeste's gift popped in her head. That could be good, enjoyable.

She flung aside the covers and pulled open the nightstand drawer for the only thing in there—the vibrator Cel had snuck into her luggage.

Cat's mouth hung open at the lifelike toy—ridges and nubs for extreme pleasure. This was a *serious* implement. Nothing like the simple one she had at home.

She stripped out of her clothes and climbed back into

bed. At first, she let her hands slide over her body, in a way Nicholas might do. Maybe.

Her nipples peaked under her touch. Her nipples were sensitive, often a simple twist would shoot straight to her clit. One hand slid south, dipping between her nether lips. She was wet, all from Nicholas's texts. From thinking about what he could do to her.

She spun the end of the vibe and it came to life. She set it against her hard nub.

Whoa! This would take some getting used to.

She clicked it off and dragged it over her sensitive lips, wetting the silicone. Her hips flexed. Oh God. This was just what she needed.

She slowly pushed the vibe inside, letting the head stimulate her G-spot. The massive implement pushed against her vaginal walls. Warmth traveled throughout her entire body.

With her other hand, she grazed a finger over her clitoris. Her inner muscles contracted and pushed against the toy. She pushed it back and nearly moaned.

Her finger worked faster, but she wanted more. If she were with a man—like Nicholas—he'd stimulate her nipples while caressing her down below. She couldn't do that for herself with only two hands.

An idea popped in her head.

She reached beside her and grabbed a large white pillow. Situating the pillow at her butt, she wedged it to hold in her vibe. Deeply set. She turned the vibe on low, then, bending her legs, her feet held the pillow in place.

Yes!

Her finger returned to her bundle of nerves while the other hand caressed her breast and played with her nipple.

Oh yes. This was exactly what she needed. Her hips rocked, mimicking the act of riding a man. Her finger circled her clit, feeling it grow under her touch. One squeeze of her nipple and electricity shot downward, lighting her up, making the vibe slip. She flexed her legs, pushing it back as deeply as it would go.

"Unh," she moaned. She was so incredibly close.

She imagined Nicholas's hands, his mouth, ravishing her. His cock deeply set inside her, claiming her for his own, wanting to please her.

The orgasm of a lifetime heightened until it exploded, radiating to every corner of Cat's body. Her back bowed off the bed as she moaned long and low, savoring the glorious climax she so desperately needed.

She collapsed and straightened her boneless legs. She pulled out her vibe, and her hands flopped to the side. *Stupendous.*

She panted until her heart stopped racing. Looking up at the ceiling she wondered where that surge of lust had come from. Her massage had definitely brought out something extraordinary... a fleeting, fanciful escapade. This? This was brought on by thoughts of Nicholas, such powerful thoughts, and God help her, she wanted them to be real. She wanted her few days on the island to be spent with him. She could do that.

She didn't need to dive into a new relationship. Heck no. But why not enjoy a little fling while she could? He'd expressed his interest in her, and she was certainly interested in him.

She set the vibe on the nightstand and clicked off the light.

Why not? It wasn't like she needed mountains of trust in the man to build a relationship on. To build happily ever after on. This would be "happy for right now."

And a fling would surely be considered *adventurous*. She smiled as she drifted off.

CHAPTER
Seven

Nic was so damn anxious to see Cat, he almost left his cell phone on the plane.

Hailing a cab, he texted Cat.

I've landed. Give me a few minutes and I'll swing by and pick u up.

She replied quickly that she would be ready.

He wondered what her day had been like, if she'd ventured off hotel property to draw with her charcoals. He made a mental note to ask if she was being taken only to safe areas. Maybe she'd gone on a tour. The resort could schedule so many fun things; Nic had tried several tours over the years. He thought of planning something for them this weekend.

Every once in a while Dillon popped in his head. If Dillon were alive today, Nic knew Cat would be the kind of woman he would tell his best friend all about.

As he arrived at her door, a small bouquet of flowers in hand, his heart pumped wildly. He'd missed her. In just a few days together, he'd become very fond of Cat and wanted to spend any free time he had together.

His dreams were filled with images of her, some where she was naked in his arms. He'd woken hard for her, and truly if he had a choice, dinner would be the last thing on their agenda tonight. But that wouldn't be right for Cat. He would just need to keep his dreams and fantasies to himself. She definitely didn't needed some jerk taking advantage of her vulnerability.

She opened the door in a pale-blue, spaghetti-strap dress. The style gently hugged her curves and the scoop neck showed just a hint of cleavage. Her dark blonde hair was pinned up and a few loose pieces framed her tanned face and slid down her bare neck. She reminded Nic of a model for a high-end women's boutique.

"Wow. You look incredible."

She bit her bottom lip. "Thank you."

With a hand on her waist, he leaned down and kissed her cheek. Her skin was soft and warm, and she smelled of a sweet, citrusy perfume. "Ready?"

She flashed her keycard and accepted his hand. He led them to a nicer restaurant than Seaside in the main building.

"Mr. Westbrook." The hostess greeted him with a smile. "Please follow me."

Right after Cat had agreed to have dinner with him, he'd called to make reservations, requesting the side with floor-to-ceiling windows. While the sun was still out, they'd get a gorgeous, uninterrupted view of the ocean.

Cat took a seat, her eyes rounded at the scene. "This is beautiful."

"Isn't it?" He sat beside her at the intimate square table. His fingers itched to touch her, but he needed to pace himself.

They perused the menu and after deciding on the chef's seafood special and ordering a bottle of white wine, Nic pivoted to face her.

"How have you been doing?"

"Well, I got to go into town yesterday and do some drawing. I think I told you the concierge put together a list of places I might like. So, I went to an old schoolhouse. It was built in the 1830s and is positively charming." Her eyes twinkled as she recounted her day.

"I should have asked you to bring your sketchbook so I could see."

A subtle blush crept over her cheeks. "Okay. Maybe later."

The waiter poured their wine, and he lifted his glass to toast her.

"And what did you do today?"

"More of the same. This time I walked to where we'd gone Monday night." She motioned her hand toward the beach. "I found a little area, like a park, and drew for a few hours."

"You really enjoy sketching."

She nodded. "I do. I sorta put it on hold when I was planning my wedding. It feels good to get back into it."

The idea that Cat could take this time and, instead of wallowing in grief, make something great of it warmed him inside. "Good for you. Do you mind me asking, are the places you go safe to be alone?"

She stopped midway from sipping her wine, perhaps surprised by his concern. "Yes. On the list, the concierge marked the best places to go by myself, and then a few where I would need accompaniment."

"Well, if I'm free, I volunteer to go with you, if you want to check out a particular spot."

She chuckled and hooked a lock of hair behind her ear. "Thanks. But I know you have to work."

He'd juggled appointments to clear his schedule just in case she was free, something he'd never done before. Their time together on the island would be short and he wanted to cram in as much as he could before she disappeared into her normal life. The way she made him feel was magical, and he'd go with it rather than make excuses. "I have a little free time built into my schedule. In fact, I was wondering if you'd like to do something this weekend."

"Oh, sure. Like what?"

"Have you ever been parasailing?"

Cat's instinct was to say no, to proceed with caution. But in truth, she thought parasailing looked exciting. She swallowed. Not only did she want to try it, she wanted to spend more time with Nicholas.

"Parasailing sounds fun," she said through a dry mouth.

His smile made her tummy flip. "Okay. I'll look into it."

Dinner was served. He had the salmon special and she'd chosen the sea scallops. Everything was fresh and delicious. She'd only been on the island a few days and already didn't want it to end.

After dinner, they lingered over the wine and chatted about his work.

"So anything interesting happen on your trip?"

He scratched his upper lip with his index finger. "Yes. I learned that one of my clients, a bar owner, intends to open another bar in the near future."

"Oh, good for him."

"Yup. And good for me." He wiggled his eyebrows. "I also learned that another customer is expecting their first baby."

"Nice."

"Why don't we take our glasses and go walk the beach?" His chin jutted toward the ocean.

With her hand in his, he led them to a vacant cabana on the sandy beach. "We can leave our shoes here, then come back and watch the waves rolls in."

She nodded.

A relaxation spread throughout her body since being on

her "honeymoon" that she couldn't define. Was it the ocean, or Nicholas? Could it have something to do with breaking up with Jack? Wasn't she supposed to be feeling miserable?

"What are you thinking about?"

She looked up at Nicholas, pulled from her deep thoughts. "I feel very relaxed, and I think it surprises me."

Nicholas nodded, gazing straight into her eyes. "I'm glad to hear that. The island can do that to a person." He grinned. "I don't mean to bring up a sore subject, but have you thought much about what it will be like when you return?"

She had, and the outlook was bleak. "Yes. I've decided to stay here for the rest of my life."

He froze for a second, his eyes widening before softening, realizing she was joking. "Oh, got me."

She chuckled. "I *have* thought about it. When I left, Jack was anxious to try and explain everything. I'm sure he'll want to try and win me back."

"And how do you feel about that?"

She shrugged a shoulder. Honestly, she didn't like thinking about the whole humiliating episode. This honeymoon—vacation, whatever—was a blessed distraction from the images of Jack and that bimbo. A break from the heartache.

At some point, she'd have to resolve what had happened once and for all.

One lesson she'd learned thus far was that maybe she'd

changed too much of her life for Jack. Her drawing was just one example.

She was thankful when Nicholas switched the subject.

They walked for some distance, passing large national hotel and resort chains, a few that Cat recognized by name.

On their way back to the resort, the sun hung low in the sky, almost as if God set it on the edge of the ocean for the world to admire. A kaleidoscope of color filled the horizon. Nicholas stopped them to watch the sun slowly dip out of sight. He stepped behind her, wrapping his arms around her torso. She bathed in the feel of his body warming hers and rested her head against his shoulder.

He pressed several small kisses against her neck. "Beautiful, isn't it?"

Her tummy fluttered as his breath floated over her skin. "Yes. Simple breathtaking."

After a few short moments, they continued their walk. She loved how inquisitive he was, how interested he was in her. It was easier to forget about Jack when they were talking about so many other things.

A strange noise lingered in the air. Cat gazed up at Nicholas—his alerted expression showed he'd heard it too.

"What is that?"

He shook his head, narrowing his eyes in concentration.

The intermittent sound, sort of a high-pitched whistle, grew louder as they walked.

At this time of night, it was hard to see much and the beach was mostly clear of vacationers as people moved inside to the nightclub and bars.

They passed a cabana with the curtains drawn and the noise returned.

A woman.

Nicholas looked down at Cat and grinned. He squeezed her hand and kept walking. Once they arrived at their resort property, they took a seat on the double-lounger where they'd left their shoes.

She brushed off her feet and leaned back, sinking into the plush cushion.

"Can I get you a drink?" he asked.

"No, thanks. I feel very content."

He assumed her same position, his thigh flush against hers.

"That was interesting," she said.

He turned toward her. "Yup—relaxation on vacation."

Her massage from earlier in the week popped into her head. "Indeed."

The gentle motion of the sea filled the moment. Moonlight bounced off the waves. "It's almost like the waves come up, grab your stress, and carry it out to sea."

Nicholas nodded and leaned close, placing a small kiss on her lips. He pulled back and smiled. "I'm so glad you're relaxed."

Mostly relaxed. Being this close to Nicholas, she

became unsettled—in a good way.

Inching closer, she laid a hand on his toned chest and kissed him—this time deeper.

His eyes opened, perhaps surprised by her actions. Eyeing the drapes, he stood and unclasped them from the wooden poles they were tied to. The drapes flowed down on each side, leaving only the view of the ocean directly before them.

He returned to her side. "Now, we can have some privacy."

She smiled. "I like kissing you." It sounded silly saying it, but it was the truth. She'd thought several times about his kisses and shocked herself that she hadn't compared them to Jack's. Maybe there was just no comparison.

With his arm bracing himself above her head, his free hand cupped the back of her neck and drew her in. The tip of his tongue tested her. She opened and let their tongues dance. He tasted faintly of wine, and she craved more. Her hands roamed his chest over his fine cotton shirt. A familiar ache built in her nether region.

What if this went too far? They were outside.

She turned to the side, breaking their kiss.

"Everything all right?" His eyebrows pulled together.

She didn't want him to think she wasn't attracted to him. "I'm nervous, I guess."

"Why? Please don't be. I love having your hands on me."

And she loved touching him. But still... She nibbled her bottom lip.

"I know you said you're not adventurous..."

She nodded.

"But we don't have to be like that couple up the beach." He motioned with his chin.

She grinned. As much as she wanted to be with Nicholas, wanted to feel his body next to hers, she wasn't an exhibitionist.

He leaned closer, laying gentle kisses along her neck and clavicle.

She rested her head back, relishing his firm mouth on her, and exhaled. His masculine scent mixed with the calming ocean waves brought down her anxiety. As his kisses traveled to her shoulder, she felt herself sinking further into the cushion.

She longed to feel his skin. Her hands reached for the buttons of his shirt to unfasten them. She explored his chest, grazing over the smattering of hair and dipping in the grooves of his abdomen.

Without a word, he pushed off the lounger to adjust the back to recline more, then returned to kissing her. He devoured her mouth and pulled her closer. His growing erection dug into her thigh.

The feeling of him being turned on by her fueled her own desire. She shifted under him to get closer. And did she get closer. Unintentionally, the apex of her thigh aligned right with his solid cock. Liquid heat filled her sex.

Oh God.

Nicholas panted in her ear. "Cat, you feel amazing. I want to kiss more of you. Please."

Night had fallen. The stars were out. It would be hard for anyone to see what they were specifically doing. Not to mention, the drapes on three sides gave good coverage.

Her pulse raced. She could do this—venture out of her comfort zone a bit. "Okay."

Cupping her jaw, Nicholas tipped her head to the side giving him access to her neck. His kisses traveled down her cheek and neck to her chest. With a small tug on her dress strap, he slid the fabric off her shoulder.

Her breath came quicker, and her breasts grew heavy.

With his free hand, he stroked her thigh, slowly sliding under her dress. His hand gripped the flesh of her ass, pulling her closer.

She moaned at the deeper contact when his cock slid over her swollen lips and clit. Her eyelids fluttered closed, savoring Nicholas's kisses.

His mouth dipped lower, skirting the edge of her bodice. She bowed her back, aching for his mouth to claim more of her.

He tore his mouth away from her chest, his eyes gleaming even in the darkness. Slowly, his fingertips glossed over the area his mouth had just set on fire and pushed the remaining strap of the dress off her shoulder. Another skate of his fingers over her chest and her dress went lower.

She knew what he was silently asking.

He lowered his mouth and slid his tongue under the edge of her dress, caressing her plump flesh, driving her to the edge of madness.

She'd never begged for anything, but somehow the urge was overwhelming right then.

With his lower hand, he bent her knee and shifted over her again.

"Mmm."

His hand massaged her ass while his cock rocked directly over her clit. Over and over, the stimulation sent the delicious sensation deeper.

Using his teeth, he tugged at her dress, revealing her breasts. Instantly, he laid claim to her nipple.

"Unh." She arched into the blessed warmth of his mouth, gripping his upper arms and shamelessly pulling herself into him. Everything felt so incredibly good, but God, she needed more.

"Cat, can you come like this? I want you to come."

Maybe, but what did that mean? How far would he go?

"I have an idea," he continued. "If you'll trust me, I want to try something that might work."

She *wanted* to trust him. She wanted him to make her come, but she wasn't ready to risk it all. Biting the inside of her cheek, she nodded twice, fully prepared to tell him to stop.

He leveraged himself up on one arm as he bent her other leg off to the side.

She lay on the lounger in a butterfly position. Slowly, he dragged her dress over her hips, exposing her wet satin thong clinging to her sex.

"Uh—"

"Hang on, Cat. Just give me a second. We can stop if you want, but no one can see you," he whispered.

His body blocked the view, and from what she could tell, not a soul had passed by the entire time.

He grazed a finger down the middle of her slit over her panties.

"Ah."

"Baby, you feel so warm and wet. One day, I'll taste you, and make you come all over my tongue."

Oh geez. That made her want it right then. To hell with being outside.

His hand reached for his pants.

She froze. She watched him unbutton his pants and lower his zipper.

"I won't, Cat. I promise."

No. True to his word, he didn't try and make love to her. Instead, he brought himself back into alignment with her nether lips. His thick cock stretched inside his soft briefs.

"Fuck, Cat." He gently rocked up and down, his cock sliding over her slit with just two thin pieces of fabric shielding them from bare contact.

"Ohmigod. That's incredible." Her eyelids slammed closed.

His lips crashed down on hers, not letting his hips stop their gentle ministrations. The ridges of his cock caressed her, even through two layers of fabric, she felt all of him stimulating her clit, causing her to climb higher.

His kisses left her mouth and headed south. "Baby, take your hands and hold those gorgeous breasts for me."

She did as he bid, offering herself to his eager mouth.

He sucked and laved at her nipples, one at a time, all while his hips gyrated over her.

God, it all felt so damn good. Her hips began to move with his rhythm.

He sucked harder and moved faster, his cock grinding against her aching clit, mimicking the act of sex.

It was hot and sexy and so insanely daring. She'd never done anything so crazy in her life. Actually, this would be the second crazy thing she'd done this week.

Never mind.

"Nicholas, don't stop. You feel so good."

He took her other breast in his mouth, sucking and biting at her nipple.

Her climax climbed to the surface, and after a few more of his thrusts, she exploded, the sensations radiating throughout her body. She almost screamed out, but his mouth swallowed her cry.

She rode the waves and was vaguely aware of the

twitching of his cock in his own release.

He collapsed to the side of her, both of them panting in exertion.

He pushed her dress down and turned her to face him, her naked breasts pressed against his bare chest. "That was crazy good."

"That... there are no words," she grinned. She should be horrified at what they'd done. Absolutely mortified. But instead she felt sated and an inexplicable relaxation fell over her, a peace and calming. Like something she'd never felt before, but Lordy she wanted to feel it again and again.

CHAPTER
Eight

Nic woke after sleeping like the dead. The night before with Cat had been nothing short of sensational. He'd gotten carried away, and knew for sure she'd jump up and run as fast as she could once she came to her senses. But praise the heavens above, she didn't. She was so damned tempting. Nic had no control when he was around her.

Her beautiful satin-clad pussy, soaked from her arousal, had been a gorgeous sight. How easy it would have been to slide those panties aside and enter her dripping wet channel.

He wondered if she would have let him, if he'd asked. But deep inside, he was glad he'd showed restraint.

Tonight. She was ready for him. He could feel it, and he couldn't wait.

Fuck! He'd dressed and had a flight departing for Puerto Rico in an hour but had a raging hard-on. No time to take care of that. He had to plow through.

On his way out, he stopped at the concierge desk to

book parasailing for the next day and dinner that night. He set the reservation time and put a few other things into motion.

Tonight would be a night she'd remember long after leaving the island, if he had his way.

Cat spoke to the front desk receptionist after breakfast and learned that the resort property was larger than she'd realized. The receptionist explained there were walking paths that ran through the garden, along another pool and a hot tub, and snaked through the entire property. A perfect place to explore.

Although she brought her sketchbook, she had one thing on her mind—she had to call Celeste.

"Ohmigosh! How are you? How's your vacation?"

Cat chuckled at her friend's enthusiasm, even as her voice sounded low and groggy.

"Hey babe. I'm sorry. Did I wake you?"

"Don't worry about that. Tell me what's going on. Been on any tours? How's the eye-candy?"

Cat meandered passed the pool and hot tub, taking in the lush tropical greenery on both sides of the path. She didn't know where to start. "Well, first, I'm drawing a lot more. I must have sketched a dozen scenes."

"Nice," Cel drew out the word.

"But that's not really the most interesting part." Cat stopped at a stone bench and sat.

"Oh, really?"

"Um, so Tuesday, I had a massage. It was... really good."

"What?! Are you kidding me?"

Cat could picture her friend bolting upright in her bed, her eyes bugging out of her head. "Ohmigosh, Cel, it was so fantastic. I can't believe it. I can't believe I let a stranger touch me like that."

"Yay you! That's just what you needed. Way to go."

Cat licked her lips. "There's something else?"

"Oh. This is getting good. Let me guess, a cabana boy?" She laughed. "No, not exactly.

"Okay, what exactly?

"I met a man. He lives in Orlando, but has to travel here for work. And he's cute and he finds me attractive. And..."

"And what?"

"He invited me to dinner last night and then for a walk along the beach. Afterward, we stopped at one of those outdoor cabanas on the beach. Gosh, he's such a good kisser. I can't even remember what Jack's kisses are like."

"Cat, that's great, but why do I get the feeling there was more? Did y'all have sex?"

A flush of heat filled her cheeks. "No, clothes were still on, but we both came."

"Wow. Who is this woman?" Celeste laughed.

"I know, this is sooo unlike me." Her eyes rounded even though her friend couldn't see. "I can hardly believe it myself. I don't know if it's Nicholas or the island or what. I'm so relaxed, and I hardly think of Jack. Is that wrong? There must be something wrong with me. I'm gonna come home and completely fall apart, aren't I?"

"Calm down. Just a second. Nothing like that is gonna happen. The fact that you aren't thinking about Jack-Ass constantly is a *good* thing."

Celeste might have a point.

"So, you like this guy. That's great. Enjoy the company while you're there."

Cat paused for a moment. "You think I should have sex with him?"

"Ha! Sounds like you're already heading in that direction." Celeste exhaled. "Cat, forget about Jack and work and Austin, all of it. Enjoy your time with this guy. Let yourself have fun. Give yourself permission to try new things."

"Okay, Cel. You're right."

Cat walked on as she chatted before Celeste had to get ready for work. She followed the path through the manicured grounds, the palm trees providing coverage from the sun. She passed several park benches and hammocks strung between trees laced with exotic, colorful flowers. Images of Nicholas continuously popped into her head. She might be falling in lust with him.

After another fifteen minutes Cat returned to the main building. She had twenty minutes before a Pilates class would start. She glanced at her planner before leaving her room. Next week was snorkeling, paddle boarding, a facial, and of course, more drawing. Aside from the parasailing, she secretly hoped Nicholas would be able to join her for an activity or two, given this would be her last week.

She caught herself counting down the hours when Nicholas would pick her up for dinner.

No, she scolded herself. *No obsessing over a man.*

This time was for her. Time to evaluate, to get clarity and perspective.

Nic had only one day in Puerto Rico, but that was all he needed. He made several stops, all of them very productive. The island as a whole had made serious strides in their recovery since the devastating hurricane a few years back. Most everyone he met had a renewed optimism about the future. As tourism improved so did the economy, including several orders he snagged that day.

He combed his work email, waiting for his flight to be called, when his cell phone rang. His sister.

"Hey, Lisa. How's it goin'?" His sister was a brilliant lawyer. She'd nailed an incredible case last month involving a professor's intellectual property and his Ivy League school employer. Bloomberg featured her on their homepage because of it.

"Good. Listen, Nic, I'm putting some plans together for

the July 4th holiday. Got a minute to talk?"

"Sure." How she had time to coordinate a mini-family reunion while running a thriving practice was completely lost on Nic. Even being married hadn't slowed her down in her practice.

He listened as Lisa rattled off plans and flight reservations for herself and her husband. She said she'd already spoken to their older brother, Samuel, who was going to block out the time. Everyone was to converge at their parents' house in the Carolina Mountains.

Nic scrolled through his calendar. It was perfectly clear of social events that weekend—as it usually was. Workaholic was his middle name.

"Okay, sis, sounds good to me. I'll look into flights and plan to be there."

"Oh, good. I was concerned since you hadn't gotten your promotion yet that you'd bail."

"Ha. Ha." She thought she was throwing salt in the wound, but he knew he was right on track for his promotion.

"Anyway, Samuel's bringing Monica, looks like it's getting serious. So feel free to bring a guest." He heard the lilt in her voice as she more-than-hinted at him bringing a girlfriend.

Cat was the first person who popped into his mind. She would fit right in with his family. They'd love her—her easy spirit, her quiet intellect, her contagious smile, all of it.

Seeing her long-term wasn't feasible—not only because

of the distance, but because of his career. What they had right now was perfect.

"I know. Thanks, sis." He disconnected the line.

Boarding started for his flight, so researching travel to his parents' house would have to wait. Hell, he had so many miles saved up, he could make the trip for free.

Cat stared at the water from her hotel room balcony. Nicholas would be there in mere minutes and her body hummed with anticipation.

After an invigorating Pilates class and then lunch, she'd sketched freely, trying to distract herself from thoughts of Nicholas. She replayed her encouraging conversation with Celeste—not that she needed her friend's permission to move forward with Nicholas. She was already more than interested in going further. He enthralled her in a way she couldn't explain.

She honestly couldn't remember this kind of craze with Jack.

She'd done some extra pampering and now felt her absolute best. Perusing through the boutique at the main building earlier she'd spied a decadent selection of thongs and purchased two pair. Panties was all she needed for that night, no bra. She glanced down at her dress—a long, flowing halter-style that cut deep, showing off her tan and gathering nicely over her boobs. It was a tad risqué for her, but considering it was already packed, she'd kept it. Now, she was glad she had. Nicholas would love it. She'd pinned her hair up in a messy twist, letting a few pieces fall haphazardly. Lastly, her makeup, although not much was needed, looked perfect, she had to admit.

A knock sounded on the door. Her stomach tumbled as she opened it.

"Hi."

"Hi." Nicholas smiled, holding her gaze before visually tracing her form. "You look beautiful."

He placed his hand at her waist and kissed her cheek, lingering.

A shiver raced down her spine. "Thank you."

He turned and offered his arm. "Ready?"

What a gentleman, she thought. "Yes."

Dinner was spectacular. They were seated in a booth tucked in a cozy corner. If she didn't know better, she'd think he'd planned this specifically.

He sat close, his leg grazing against hers. His touches were driving her mad—little caresses on her thigh, small circles over the back of her hand with his fingertips. He charmed her with his compliments, and his eyes smiled at her, never breaking his gaze—like she was the only person in the room.

Near the end, he leaned in. "Would you like to come back to my room for a nightcap?"

She felt the heat rise to her chest and cheeks. "That

would be lovely."

After dinner, he held her hand, guiding her away from the main building to the elevator and to his room.

She walked into a suite similar to her own with a tray of chocolate-covered strawberries, a bottle of liqueur, and two crystal glasses sitting on the table. Scattered in a few places were white votive candles not yet lit. He *had* made plans.

"How about we go out on the balcony?"

She crossed the room to the narrow veranda. The sun was several minutes away from setting over the blue sea.

He joined her, offering her a glass. "Cheers."

She smiled and sipped the sweet liqueur. "Mmm. Delicious."

He held her gaze, then turned to face the water. "Great view isn't it?"

"It is." She inhaled and took another sip. "Do you live far from the ocean?" Cat glanced toward him.

He shrugged. "Nope, maybe an hour drive to Cocoa Beach. But I'm not much for downtime."

She thought all men lived for vacations and getaways. Time to blow off steam. Cat tipped her head. "Really?"

"I guess you could say my vacations happen during work." He flashed a wide, white smile.

She chuckled, then turned back to the sunset.

Nicholas placed his glass on the little bistro table and stepped behind her. "Did I tell you that you look beautiful?" He kissed the side of her neck.

"Mm-hm."

His hands caressed her bare arms as he kept kissing her neck and shoulder. "Good, because you do. You make this dress look like a million bucks," he whispered.

She smiled, and her eyelids fell closed, savoring his kisses.

After a few moments, he said, "Take another sip, Cat, and hand me your glass."

She did as he bid, acutely aware of the wetness that gathered at the apex of her thighs.

His lips returned to their sweet assault, and his hands smoothed over her hips and lower back. "Your skin is so soft." He slid his hands higher, up her exposed back, to her dress clasp.

Her breath quickened.

"Cat, may I unclip this so I can keep kissing your neck?"

Her heart skipped a beat.

He didn't wait for a reply.

Her hands grabbed the front of the dress above her boobs, preventing the dress from falling.

Nicholas peeled away the strap ends, kissing her newly exposed skin. His kisses sent a sizzling hot trail over her body, awakening something deep inside in her.

His hands snuck under the fabric to her tummy.

She was nearly panting now.

She closed her eyes, only to have them fly open when his hands crept higher. "Nicholas."

"Cat, I only want to make you feel good. It's okay. No one can see."

She looked to the right and the left. No one was out on their balconies. The other guests were probably at the bar or in town.

His hands covered both breasts, under her dress.

"Oh God," she breathed.

"Shit, Cat. You feel so good. I've been thinking about being alone with you all day."

He caressed her breasts and stroked her nipples. His forefinger and index finger toyed with them, which drove her positively insane. His erection pressed into her.

Her head lulled back against his shoulder as she pushed further into his hands, all while she had a death-grip on her dress.

His hand snaked down and back to the dress's zipper.

Her heartrate sped as her eyes darted again. *What if someone sees us?*

He unfastened the short zipper, loosening the fabric. "Relax, beautiful. I won't do anything more out here. I promise."

She took in a shallow breath and allowed his roaming hands to pull her back onto his sensuous ride. His seductive kisses and touches made Cat unravel the last thread of discretion. His hand slid over her new silky panties to her mound and drew out a moan. She bit her lip, anxious for him to touch her clitoris but equally anxious to get back into the room, into privacy.

His hand left her breast to grab her neck, aligning his lips with hers. She opened for him to dive in, his tongue tangling with hers as his fingertips danced over her mound, neglecting her most-eager clit.

God, was she crazy to want him to touch her, under her panties? Out here?

He broke the kiss, roaming her neck, gently sucking as he pushed away the two loose ends of her dress off her neck. One hand reclaimed her breast, the other only caressed her low belly.

"Nicholas." She panted.

"Yes?"

Words wouldn't come.

"I promised you no more, but I would happily give you something more, beautiful. Do you need more?"

Oh God, yes. Could she? She bit her lip. Her mind spun in uncertain circles. "Yes," she finally whispered.

A fingertip slid under her waistband, teasing back and forth before dipping into her warm crevice.

"Oh God."

Then he dipped a little lower gathering some lubrication to run over her swollen clit. He massaged and circled, gently adding pressure.

She separated her legs several inches. She couldn't believe it. She was letting him bring her to orgasm out here. After what she'd experienced so far on this trip, she shouldn't be surprised.

She wished she could let her arms down, but she didn't dare.

A familiar sensation bubbled up, and Nicholas didn't relent. Her hips flexed forward, wanting just what he so expertly gave her.

"Ah."

"Yes, Cat. Please come on my fingers."

She exploded, an intensity shot through her, making her knees go weak.

Nicholas tightened his hold across her mid-section, keeping her upright, riding out the waves that crashed through her.

"You all right?" he spoke softly.

Her chest heaved. "Yes," she managed.

He pecked the top of her shoulder. "Cat," several more pecks, "I love feeling you come. I would love to strip you out of this dress and do it again."

She'd love anything and everything he gave her, but not here. No way. "Let's go inside."

CHAPTER
Nine

Cat was incredible; there was no two ways about it. Feeling her writhe under his touch as she spiraled into orgasm was phenomenal. Her sweet soft body, so ripe for his dick to slide into, made him want to lift her dress right there. But Nic knew that would be pushing her too far too fast.

He pulled his hands out from under her dress and coaxed her inside. He closed the glass door and turned to find her standing beside the bed, both hands gripping her dress close to her chest.

He stepped before her, cupped her face, and claimed her pretty mouth. Her soft lips drove him crazy. "Cat, take off my shirt," he whispered over her mouth.

Her sight bolted to the window, then back at him. "Aren't you going to close the drapes?"

He knew he pushed her, hard, against her super protective boundaries. He didn't bother to look back. "It's almost dark. And being on the sixth floor, no one can see."

She licked her precious pink lips and slowly released

the hold on her dress. It crumbled to the carpet, and she stepped out. She stood before him in panties, heels, and earrings. Gorgeous.

Cat unbuttoned his shirt with tentative movements, slowly becoming more sure, and she didn't stop there. With a quick glance up at him, she started on his belt. His button and zipper were next. She pushed his pants off his hips.

He toed off his shoes and yanked off his socks and shirt, leaving everything in a pile on the floor.

Her hands skated over his chest, stomach, and down to his cock.

He loved her touching him, but he was too close to blowing his wad—he had to stop her. He leaned down to claim one of her hard pink nubs, drawing it into his mouth.

She mewled.

He drew in the other nipple, loving how responsive her nipples were. He'd remember that.

With an arm around her waist, he backed up to the bed, slowly lowered her, and slid her to the center of the mattress—his mouth on hers one last time before he headed for his destination.

His kisses traveled from her succulent breasts to her smooth stomach to the little piece of fabric called panties. "These are pretty," he murmured over her mound, laying a kiss directly on top.

"Unh. I just bought them."

He peered up at her.

Her lips curled at the corners. "For you."

That pleased him. He smiled and glanced down again. Now to try and push just a bit more.

He hooked two fingers under the white confection, and as she raised her hips, he drew the panties down her legs, careful to leave on her high heels. Then taking her right leg, bending it, he placed her foot on the bed out to the side.

Her eyes went wide, and she swallowed.

He proceeded to the left leg, repeating the process.

She lay before him, legs bent and open, naked save for her shoes. A pale brown strip of hair led him exactly where he wanted to feast.

He rubbed a hand over his aching, hard-as-steel dick. "Fuck, Cat. You look so delectable." He knelt on the bed between her legs, leaning down to kiss her.

She clasped the back of his neck, kissing him with equal vigor.

Damn! How he wanted to fuck her.

He whispered over her lips. "I can't wait to taste you. When I'm done I'm gonna fuck you, baby. I want to feel you around me when I come. I have a condom."

She didn't hesitate and nodded. Her beautiful eyes were a deep emerald color.

He rose, whipped off his underwear, and retrieved a condom from the nightstand. One last glance, he saw her sweet cream spilling from her pussy. Kneeling down, he took her pussy like a man who hadn't eaten in a decade.

"Unh," she cried out.

Ah fuck, his girl was ready to come again.

He licked up her center, over and around her clit, toying with the tiny bud, then poked into her channel.

"Nicholas."

He ate her while her hips gently rocked beneath him. He amped up his pressure and speed, and less than a minute later, she was coming.

"Ah, Nicholas. Ah."

Oh, yes, baby.

She squirmed some more, and when he knew she was done, he sheathed his aching dick with a condom.

"Please, Nicholas." Her outstretched arms reached for him.

"You got it, baby." He knelt on the bed, one arm lifting her waist, and dove into her slick, hot pussy.

Her eyelids fluttered closed as she bowed off the bed and moaned.

He didn't know how long he would last, but he could probably be ready for round two in a few minutes. His thrusts were deep and long, and he could see her clamped lips preventing her from screaming out. He wanted to hear her, but maybe next time. He rammed once more before blasting through the walls he'd fortified for the last thirty minutes.

He growled and collapsed over her warm body, panting into her shoulder. Once their breathing returned, he walked to the bathroom and pitched the condom.

He returned to find Cat exactly as he'd left her. That made him smile. There was so much he knew he could show her, so much he could bring out of her. Not to be egotistical about it. No, this was about pure joy and mutual satisfaction.

Clasping one ankle at a time, he removed her sexy heels, then yanked a sheet over them as he lay beside her.

She turned to face him, cheeks flushed pink, smiling.

"Cat, I understand if you want to go back to your room, but I would love to have you stay. Stay the whole night. If it's all right with you, I want to do that again."

Her smile widened. "I would like to do that again, but later I should go back to my room."

"Okay, I can walk you whenever you're ready. I'm going to get our drinks."

He walked outside, naked—but who the fuck really cared?—and carried back in their glasses. "Tomorrow, we have parasailing at ten a.m."

She sat up, drinking nearly half of what remained.

He chuckled. "You nervous?"

"Uh-huh."

"Don't be, it'll be great." He tried reassuring her with a pat on her thigh. *If* she could trust him enough to let go, his safe, cautious Cat was in for a treat—tomorrow and the rest of her stay here. She could take a chance on some fun and forget about the asshole who'd cheated on her. Well, forget about him if Nic had any say on the matter.

She and Nicholas were next to go up in the parasail. Her heart slammed into her ribs.

"What scares you?" He looked at her with amused concern in his eyes.

"It's like I'm a kite. Any kite I ever had just did a nosedive."

He smiled. "Well, that's not gonna happen here. Balloons and parasails act differently than kites."

She tried thinking of a good excuse to bail. Really she'd been thinking about an excuse since he'd brought up the idea the prior day. She didn't want to chicken out, but this activity didn't seem very safe. Her palms grew sweaty.

"Don't overthink it," he leaned in, whispering in her ear. "It'll be great."

A crew member in a bright yellow shirt clicked the last buckle on her life jacket, then he instructed them to sit at the back of the boat. More buckling happened.

Nicholas squeezed her hand. "I'll be great, babe."

They were given some final instructions, but all Cat could do was try and breathe as she gripped the straps holding her to the canopy.

"Ready?" the guy asked, and Nicholas nodded.

It all happened so fast. The air simply pulled them off the back of the boat as they lifted higher into the sky, the boat racing forward in the water.

"Ah!" she cried out, watching the distance grow

between her and the boat, feeling nothing beneath her.

They climbed higher and faster.

"Ohmigosh! I am really high. We're really high. Our boat is so tiny."

Nicholas grinned at her.

"Okay. I'm okay. We're just gonna float along... above the earth." She inhaled, and glanced at him. "How are you so calm?"

"This is exciting, isn't it? Look out at the horizon."

As they climbed higher and finally stopped, Cat scanned everything below. Every boat seemed so small, the vastness of the blue ocean stretched below them. She could see buildings, but cars and people were much harder.

After her heartrate slowed, she could appreciate the view. The wondrous earth that lay before their eyes. Moments like this showed her just how small she was, a tiny drop in a massive bucket.

"Cool, isn't it?"

She nodded, unable to find the energy to make her mouth move. It was empowering and humbling at the same time being this high above the ground. If she felt so small, why weren't her problems so small too? Wishful thinking.

"This *is* cool." She cracked a smile for the first time all day.

Several minutes passed and she felt the tug on the line as they were pulled in.

"We have to hold on to the passenger bar now,"

Nicholas said as his hands reached overhead.

She followed suit, and breathed through the action of being reeled in closer to the boat.

They landed—because that was really the only word to describe it—back on the boat. Adrenaline coursed through her veins.

After the life jackets were off, she looked up at Nicholas and swung her arms around his neck. "I did it. I can't believe I did it. That was so exciting. The most exciting thing I've ever done."

He chuckled in her hair, holding her close.

She loved the feel of his arms wrapped around her. She pecked his cheek.

"I'm glad you liked it," he whispered.

She grinned the whole rest of the boat ride.

They had nothing else planned for the remainder of the day. They could just lounge around, nap, make love, whatever they wanted. And that sounded just perfect to Cat. She had no problem spending her free time with Nicholas.

After they docked, she mustered the strength to invite Nicholas back to her room, and then asked him if he wanted to shower with her. Somehow her newfound gumption was growing and taking her places.

They lounged by the pool after lunch, then made love again before dinner.

Cat almost felt like Nicholas just couldn't get enough of her. She'd never dated a man who was like that. Not that they were dating. But the day was simply wonderful. She had one week left and the way things were going, those days would be spectacular.

Nic sat across from Cat, watching her laugh as the juice from a cherry tomato dribbled down her chin.

She dabbed with a napkin. "So how many times have you been parasailing?"

He still felt so full of pride that Cat was able to trust him enough to go on their excursion. "Only about three or four times."

She nodded. "Do you do other things like that?"

She was too adorable in her innocence, considering parasailing adventurous. What would she think if she knew just how adventurous he was?

He set down his fork. "Yes. You might call me a risk-taker. I've gone hang gliding, swam with sharks, bungee jumped, and parachuted out of an airplane."

Her mouth hung open. "Holy cow."

He grinned and took a bite of his salad.

"Have you always been this way?"

He didn't often talk about Dillon, but just as she could step out of her comfort zone, so could he. "A few years ago, I lost my best friend in a freak accident."

"Ohmigosh. I'm so sorry."

Nic inhaled. "He worked for a manufacturing company.

He went to the plant early one morning for an inspection when a propylene tank exploded. Thankfully no one else had arrived yet. Dillon always lived life to the fullest." A small smile spread across his lips. "Making the most of every day." It was almost like he knew his life would be cut short. "And that's what I learned from him."

"Wow. What a story." She reached across the table to squeeze his hand.

He could read sincerity in her eyes, and he loved how she cared. Then a glint sparked. "So, you're pretty much a daredevil."

"That works. I'm a bit competitive too." He undoubtedly had Lisa and Samuel to thank for that. "I like to think that life's too short to have regrets."

She nodded and looped a stray lock of hair behind her ear.

The waitress arrived with their entrees.

Perfect time to change the subject. "So, besides drawing, what were you planning on doing this vacation? Did you book any excursions?"

The corners of her lips rose. "I didn't plan *too* much. I'll go paddle boarding and snorkeling this week."

He sipped from his wine glass.

"What? That sounds really 'safe' to you, doesn't it?"

Now it was his turn to reach for her hand. "It does. But Cat, I'm really proud of you for taking a chance and parasailing with me today. And you should be proud of yourself."

She pushed her shoulders back. "I am. I'm surprised how much I liked it."

He couldn't stop the smile at her own delight.

They chatted nonstop over dinner. He simply couldn't believe how much of his free time he was spending with her. Not that he regretted it. They'd formed an easy friendship— friends with benefits.

After dinner, he walked her back to her room and didn't leave for two hours.

She wore a sexy, matching pink bra and panties under her dress that night, saying they were a bridesmaid's present.

He had only one reply. "Those bra and panties look amazing on you. I wonder how they'll look on the floor."

She giggled as he unclasped her bra and ravaged her body.

Cat was good and caring and innocent in many ways. The ideas were already swirling around in his head of all the wonderful things he could show her. Take it easy, he reminded himself.

CHAPTER
Ten

Cat toweled off the last of the water drops from her shower and squeezed the excess from her hair. She stared at her reflection as she combed her locks smooth, reminiscing about the fabulous weekend she'd had. What a difference a few days could make. She didn't know where this fling with Nicholas was going; likely not very far. But she'd learn to live with that. She had a fresh perspective on life and love, and frankly lust.

It might have been rough the prior week, but Jack had done her a huge favor by cheating. It was a blessing that she'd found Jack, that he hadn't replied to her texts that fateful night. She'd almost married the wrong man because no way in hell would he *not* cheat on her when they were married.

She would be eternally thankful to Nicholas for showing her another side of life.

As she swept some coconut-scented lotion over her legs a knock sounded at the door.

She glanced at her phone. Nearly nine o'clock.

Looking through the peephole, she saw Nicholas freshly shaven and wearing a pale green logoed shirt and khaki pants.

Her heart skipped a beat. She tightened the sash on her robe and pulled open the door. "Hi, stranger."

"Good morning, beautiful," he said with a wide smile.

She stepped back to let him in. "I wasn't expecting to see you until tonight."

He snaked an arm around her waist and leaned forward to kiss her cheek. "I know. I'm sorry but I need to cancel dinner tonight. One of my appointments got moved from this morning, so I thought I'd take you to breakfast instead."

"Wow, okay. Let me get some clothes on."

His gaze traveled the length of her. "Are you very hungry right now?"

Oh my. She licked her lips. Clearing her throat, she replied, "No."

His hands stroked up her arms over her soft cotton robe, leaving a trail of warmth on her skin. He lowered his head to her lips, testing. She opened for him, savoring the feel of his minty tongue sliding against hers.

He pulled her flush to his body, his heat radiating across her entire front. His fingertips grazed up her neck, and his head tipped to deepen the kiss.

Clasping his upper arms, she pressed her body against his, loving the feel of his erection digging into her. Her breasts grew heavy, aching for his touch.

He stepped back, and slowly drew his fingers down the V of her robe, waiting for her to object.

She wouldn't. The tension in her sex built and wetness accumulated. His confidence sparked a new awareness in her, and her body responded to his touch like he was put on this earth to please her.

He slipped out the knot of her sash, peeled the fabric apart, and it cascaded to the floor.

"Holy fuck, Cat."

Her nipples pinched into hard nubs under his stare.

His hands cupped the sides of her breasts, his thumb toying with her nipples, before he lowered to take one into his mouth. He laved and sucked on them like they were candy.

"Unh." Her head fell back as she relished his attention.

He rose, his eyes a deep ocean-blue. "I want to taste you, Cat. Let's try something new."

She was hesitant, but more anxious to learn what he had in mind. "Okay."

He pulled off his shirt and draped it over the dresser.

Like a magnet, her hands flew to his muscular chest—solid, warm, and all male.

He lifted her hands off and kissed the palms. "Come this way."

He led her a few steps to the end of the bed, facing it. His hands stroked her hips and thighs, then up her torso to her breasts. He placed kisses on her neck, biting gently.

She moaned, and her head lolled back against his shoulder.

"Your body is made to be worshipped. I want to do that now. Okay?"

She knew by the way he asked he was coaxing her to try something new. Nicholas had a way of doing that. As much as her nerves rattled, she loved how he stretched her comfort zone, making her take new risks. Risks that always seemed to be more pleasurable than she could have imagined.

She exhaled. "Okay."

"Get on the bed on all fours."

She crawled unhurriedly and heard the rustling of clothes. She glanced back to see him stripping off the rest of his clothes. His naked form was glorious.

He knelt behind her, stroking and kissing her back. His hands swept to her front and played with her hard nipples. His warm breath sent tingles down her spine.

A trickle of wetness slid along the inside of her thigh. She was desperate to have him fill her.

He caressed her front, moving to her hips and thighs. "I'm going to make you come, baby. Get low, lay your head on the mattress."

She hesitated a brief second, but did as he bid, hyperaware that her backside was open to him. She felt embarrassed and emboldened at once.

"Relax," he cooed. "You look so beautiful right now, I

could come just from the sight of you and breathing in your scent."

His finger smoothed over her lower lips.

"Baby, I can see your cream. You want me inside, don't you?"

"Yes. Yes," she breathed.

"Soon." With his hands on her thighs, he lowered himself and slid his tongue through her slit.

"Oh." Her face grew warmer, and her heart raced. She ached for relief.

He did it again. "You taste amazing. Spread your legs wider for me, baby."

She moved her knees on the bed, going as wide as she comfortably could.

"That's perfect." His tongue caressed her sex again, poking into her core, lapping at her, and circling her swollen clit. His hot hands continued massaging the back of her thighs, moving to her ass cheeks.

Every lick, every touch, made her want to beg for more. She wanted to beg for him to never stop, but also beg for him to put her out of her misery. She couldn't remember a time when she needed to come so badly. How much more could she take?

He made love to her sex, building the ecstasy, but not enough to tip her over. His tongue lapped and kissed her lips as he slowly pushed a finger into her channel.

She groaned loudly.

As he stroked her wet core, his kisses traveled upward, kissing and licking her ass cheeks, moving *very* close to the center, close to her tiny hole. Her muscles contracted.

"Easy, baby. Relax." A hand stroked her torso up and down. "Let me pleasure you." His mouth returned to her ass cheek, sucking gently at first, then harder. No doubt leaving a mark.

As his tongue moved closer, she panted like she'd run a marathon.

His tongue glossed over her tight hole just when he pushed a second finger into her sex.

"Oh, God." What an amazing sensation.

He licked her again and again. The sensation was out of this world. How could something like this feel so insanely good? It made no sense, but she couldn't think about it anymore. She sucked in more air, delirious on the sensation, savoring the slow steady climb of her orgasm.

His fingers twisted and pumped inside her, and his thumb spun her clit in slow circles, all while his tongue stroked over her tiny hole.

"Ah," she cried out, and the climax she was so desperate for exploded with such intensity she felt she could pass out. "Nicki!"

He continued until her tremors subsided; he pulled back, and she collapsed flat on the bed, gasping for air.

She vaguely heard the condom wrapper and glanced up to see him sheath himself. He met her eyes. His fingers entered his mouth, and he licked them clean.

Holy cow!

He laid on the bed, pulling her to her side, and spooned her from behind.

"I want to make you come like that every chance I get. You're beautiful when you come."

"I felt like a..." She didn't want to say it. She didn't want to mention that was the exact thing she'd witnessed with Jack and the Blonde Bimbette.

He slid his arm between her breasts, cupping her neck. He angled his body, looking down at her. "What you felt like was a hot woman, exploring her sexuality. Stretching her comfort zone. What it felt like was incredible."

He was right.

She stared into his eyes and smiled. She was surrounded by his warmth, his tender hands, and he made her feel respected, not like a bimbo. She sighed.

He caressed her hip, lifted her top leg, and aligned his cock at her entrance, pushing easily through her slickness. The delicious fullness of his cock inside her made her tremble. He held her gaze as he continued his push-pull inside her.

Her eyes drifted closed.

"Baby, look at me. Look at me while I fuck you."

Oh, his words. She hardly ever used those words. But now, coming from him, she somehow loved them.

They moved as one, him rocking her gently, letting the

sensation build again.

How was that possible? She'd just come a few moments earlier.

He brought a finger to her clit and massaged it as he thrust into her pussy.

"Ooh." She knew he was going to give her another orgasm. She never had more than one at a time.

"That's right, sweetheart." His pace increased. "Now say it again."

What? She panted, trying to get oxygen to her brain. "Say what?"

"Call my name."

"Nicholas."

He shook his head. "That's not what you said when I was making you come while licking your ass."

"Oh... oh, God... I... I can't remember." Her orgasm was so close. Heaven help her. "Nicki," she blurted.

"That's right, sweetness." He pushed harder, rocking her wildly as his finger circled over her needy clit.

"Unh."

Sweat beads gathered over his brow. "You're so beautiful and you feel so good. Come with me, baby."

"Ah," she called out. "Nicki," she nearly screamed as another fierce orgasm ripped through her core and rocketed her entire being.

Nicholas growled as he pushed several more times before collapsing down behind her, his breathing heavy like hers.

"I can't think," she whispered.

He chuckled. "Good. You don't have to." With his arm wrapped around her, they laid together in amicable silence, enjoying the after-sex glow.

Finally, he lifted on his elbow to look down at her. "I can honestly say it's been a long time since I've enjoyed sex so much."

She giggled. "I've never had sex this good."

"Well, I'm glad I'm able to give that to you." He pecked her lips. "Would you mind if I rinse off in the shower before breakfast?"

"Help yourself. I'll try and make myself presentable."

He leaned down and kissed her longer. "Baby, you could go down there just like this and be *more* than presentable."

She grinned. How did he do that? How did he make her feel like she was the most beautiful woman in the world? She wasn't. Sure, she had some nice attributes, but her boobs could be perkier, maybe her hips a little curvier. When she was all made up—dress, heels, all of it—she was like an eight. Nicholas treated her like she was a ten.

That was one thing, she admitted, she would miss after they each went their separate ways. His compliments.

CHAPTER
Eleven

Cat daydreamed over breakfast about the love making she'd had with Nicholas the prior day, how intimately he'd licked and kissed her. The intensity of her orgasm surprised and shocked her. Frankly, this entire trip shocked the hell out of her. She chuckled into her coffee cup.

Nicholas had appointments on Dominica and wouldn't return until dinner that night. Tuesday.

She was closing in on her departure date and dreaded it. Her time on Saint Lucia was like a real-life fantasy. It was only temporary, yet she couldn't help but want it to go on.

Wasn't that always the case with vacations?

Ah, but this vacation—this vacation-cum-summer-fling—brought things to a whole new level.

She had no doubt she'd miss Nicholas when she returned home, but she wouldn't regret a single moment of these two weeks. Not one.

She smiled again as she stared out across the pool and patio to the ocean in no hurry since there were several hours before her facial.

The waiter reached to clear her plate. "Can I get you anything else, Miss?"

"Yes, please. Could I have an ice water to go?"

After she had her ice water, she grabbed her sketch pad and charcoals, and made her way to the valet. She took the car ride into town in search of an old church she'd read about.

When the driver stopped, Cat's jaw dropped. A beautiful stone church with its huge wooden door, tall steeple, and iron fence took her breath away.

"Thanks," she told the driver.

She found a comfortable spot across the street under a shady tree to sketch. There was so much detail in the building, she wanted to capture it all. She knew already that she'd have to come back another day to finish. No way would she rush this one.

After several hours, her stomach growled ferociously at her. Her driver arrived. Feeling incredibly accomplished, she had just enough time to get a bite, shower, and head to the spa.

She arrived at the spa, sans makeup, and the memories of last week's massage popped in her mind. Little could she know that had been the beginning of something extraordinary. She lowered her head to hide her smile as she approached the receptionist.

"Catherine Dalton, here for my four o'clock facial."

"Yes, Miss Dalton, please follow me."

She followed the woman whose nametag read Josephine. Cat hadn't noticed the short skirt of the woman's black and white uniform last week. She was fairly certain most places in the States would have more conservative attire for their employees.

Josephine opened the door to a quiet, small room, all set up with a reclining leather chair, a floor lamp, and multiple bottles of lotions and creams on a counter.

"Please slip off your top and bra and wrap this towel around you. Alesha will be right in." Josephine quietly closed the door behind her.

Cat changed and sat on the chair when Alesha walked in.

"G'afternoon, Miss Dalton," Alesha said in a heavier Lucian accent than most of the workers at the resort. Her eyes sparkled when she smiled, and she wore the same black and white mini-dress uniform as Josephine that showed off her toned legs.

"Hello. Cat, please."

"Cat, lie back, get comfortable, and I can have a good look at your skin."

Cat relaxed and Alesha reclined the chair. Taking a seat behind her head, Alesha positioned an illuminated magnifying glass close to Cat's skin. She investigated and placed small touches on Cat's forehead, cheeks, neck, and upper chest. "Beautiful skin. I see a bit of dryness and your acid mantle is low. Do you have a toner with you?"

Cat couldn't be sure with the woman's accent, but thought she'd asked about toner. That was one thing Cat had forgotten to pack. "No, I forgot it."

"Oh, no problem, dear. Let's get your skin in tip-top condition." Alesha lowered the lights and applied a cleansing cream, moving in gentle, circular motions. Her touch was instantly soothing. She stroked up the column of Cat's neck, whispering praises about how soft her skin was.

It struck Cat how congenial and polite everyone was at the resort. No one tried to call her Mrs. Sumners, no one thought her requests for travel or food or whatever were too unusual. It was truly like every employee had the sole job of making every guest feel comfortable and welcome. Maybe, for a future vacation, she could come back here. Maybe with Celeste. That made her smile unbidden.

"You have a pretty smile, Cat," Alesha whispered still diligently working.

"Thank you." She kept her eyes closed.

In a short minute, Alesha spoke again. Cat had drifted into a tranquil state and couldn't quite make out what she'd said. Something about décolletage.

Cat didn't know what to say so she just nodded. "Mm-hm."

Alesha loaded her fingertips with more cleansing cream and moved to Cat's upper chest. Her caresses and pressure were excellent. Then Alesha loosened the towel and peeled down the fabric to reveal her breasts.

Cat's eyes flew open.

"Please, Cat. Please relax and enjoy."

Cat swallowed hard and closed her eyes, trying not to appear like a prude. Perhaps this was how facials were done in the Caribbean. She let the woman do her job—there was no reason to think her facial would be anything less than spectacular. She pressed her lips together and then released a breath.

Soon, Alesha used a warm washcloth to remove the cleanser. Next another cream, something with a fruity smell, smoothed over her face. Alesha made small circles over her forehead, cheeks, sliding over and under her nose, then down the front of her neck. More lotion was applied. Alesha made full circles over Cat's breasts and up the middle as if she'd done this a million times.

Another warm cloth removed the tingly lotion, and then Alesha said something about a face mask.

The cool cream settled onto Cat's face, down her neck and circled her entire breast. Cat's mouth went dry. The woman was just doing her job, but ever so slightly, Cat was getting aroused. Alesha probably had no idea how sensitive Cat's nipples were as she glossed over them with the concoction.

The woman finished the application and moved a warm steam machine over her face, creating a soothing effect.

Cat heard Alesha shift, perhaps getting more lotion,

and then her hand reached for Cat's arm. The woman worked lotion all up and down her forearm, bicep, and triceps.

She was getting a little massage in addition to the facial. She sank deeper into a relaxed state as Alesha worked for several minutes before moving to her other arm, replicating the process.

Soon, the steam was pushed away and a warm cloth was placed over her face, except for her nose. Another was placed over her entire chest.

Alesha was gentle but thorough, wiping off any last bit of mask. She had several more steps—toner and different lotions. Each time Cat's breasts received the same treatment as her face. At one point, Alesha whispered something about "needing to dry." And instead of touching her face, she reached to her chest. Her hands were loaded with a slick, almost an oil, lotion, and Alesha massaged her chest and shoulders, and of course, returned to her breasts.

Cat felt the subtle moisture accumulate at the apex of her thighs but was too embarrassed—or maybe too relaxed—to say anything.

Alesha pushed the towel down further, moving it out of the way, and added more lotion to continue with the massage. This time she paid special attention to Cat's nipples, caressing, working in the lotion.

Oh God.

Cat's breathing increased, and unknowingly she arched

her back.

Alesha's fingertips wrapped around Cat's ribcage, covering more surface area—up to her armpits across the clavicle, into her valley, and around her breasts. Several times she repeated this movement.

Cat didn't know how long the massage went on, but she knew if the woman had volunteered to help her relieve her ache, Cat just might agree.

And that shocked her to her core. What was it with this island?

Cat wasn't some promiscuous woman. Just the opposite, according to her ex. She certainly wasn't interested in women in that way. But something about the whole experience made her want more.

Alesha gently covered her breasts with the towel and returned to applying eye cream and a sunblock. "You are a very sensuous woman, Cat."

What? Really? Cat wasn't so sure about that.

The hour had passed quickly, but the facial was wonderful.

"You can dress and I'll meet you at reception, okay?"

Cat nodded. "Thank you."

After she'd dressed and headed to the front, Alesha waited to show her a toner that would be perfect for her skin. So, of course, she bought it and left an extra tip.

She thanked Alesha and headed out. She had only one thing on her mind—to find Nicholas. Hopefully he was back from his appointments.

Nic tipped the porter for bringing the heavy box in and leaving it near the door. When Nic had long trips like this, he'd arrange for more sample bottles to be shipped to his hotel to cut down on all he had to bring with him. By the end, he usually went through everything he'd brought or had shipped, and any remaining bottles he'd just leave with his customers, and sometimes with the hotel staff.

He'd just set down his phone and keycard when someone pushed the door open behind the porter.

Cat.

"Hi. What a nice surprise." Smiling, he watched as she closed the door behind her and made the few steps toward him.

Her hands cupped the sides of his face then she rose to her toes and planted a big kiss on his lips. She paused and returned for more.

He opened for her, amazed as hell at the way she'd approached him—but not the least bit upset.

His tongue melted in the warmth of her mouth, and his hands gripped her hips, pulling her against his growing erection. His cock quickly grew to full size, ready for anything Cat needed from him at that moment.

Her hands roamed south, not bothering with his shirt, but instead went to work on unfastening his pants.

He returned the favor, stripping her out of her shirt and shorts as quickly as he could.

She broke the kiss and stepped back to toss her lingerie. With a hand on his waistband she pulled him toward the pristine white bed. "Nicki. Please." She sat on the bed, slid to the center, and laid down, reaching for him. Completely naked.

So fucking enticing.

Something happened. He didn't know what, but it must have been big. He could already see how her pussy glistened and how plump her clit looked.

He pushed out of his pants and yanked the nightstand drawer open, then ripped open a condom and covered himself. He took position over his eager woman, aligned his cock at her entrance and dove in. They moaned in unison. Her neck arched.

He drove deeper, and angling his body to one side, he circled over her hard nub.

She shrieked and grabbed his face for another deep kiss.

He pumped as he caressed her clit, anxious to give her exactly what she seemed to need.

In just a few short moments, she pulled away, bowed her head back, and moaned long and low. Her beautiful clit twitched under his fingertip. He pumped several more times, allowing his own release. Fucking incredible.

He collapsed to the side, panting from the unexpected

attack. He chuckled.

Facing each other, she smiled and laughed too.

He gripped her hand, enjoying the closeness. After another minute, he broke the silence. "That was surprising." He faced her. "Wonderful," he waggled his eyebrows, "but surprising. To what do I owe this visit?"

Her cheeks bloomed with color "I'm sorry." She reached for the edge of the cover to pull over herself.

He turned on his side. "Don't be. Please. I loved it."

She gave him a sly smile and glanced up at him through her lashes. "I had a facial."

That explained the sheen over her face and the minimal makeup.

"I... it was very unusual."

He tipped his head, curious but waiting for her to continue.

"Well, the aesthetician did my face and neck, working down to my chest. My whole chest."

Nic lifted his eyebrows and his cock came back to life.

"It was great, relaxing and all that, but I think I got aroused."

"You think?" He grinned.

She ducked to hide her smile.

With a finger under her chin, he raised her head to meet his gaze. "I'm so glad you got to experience that. That it brought you such pleasure. *And* I'm glad you came right here." He glanced down at her pretty tits and cupped one in his hand, running a thumb over her nipple. "Your nipples are sensitive. Did they harden like this when she touched them?"

Cat's breathing picked up speed. "Yes." Her eyelids fluttered closed.

Nic was fucking hard again, picturing Cat laying back, enjoying the caress of a woman. Fuck! What he wouldn't give to see that. "Your breasts *are* delicious."

He situated himself over her, claiming a ripe nipple in his mouth while he toyed with the other. After getting his woman ready for him again, he stopped and whipped off the condom. He wrapped it in a tissue, then sheathed himself, not hesitating to dive into her for round two.

"Oh God." Her hands gripped his biceps.

He loved how she moaned and sighed, how her nipples peaked, how her musky scent filled the air. Her ex was a fuckwad to have given her up.

Nic had her to himself for the rest of the week. And even if it meant juggling appointments or sacrificing sleep, he had enough time to show her just how adventurous she really could be.

CHAPTER
Twelve

Wednesday, Nic picked up the phone to invite Cat to dinner. "Why don't we do the grill tonight?" There was an inexplicable easiness they'd built quickly, and frankly he liked it.

"Sounds great."

"And bring your sketchbook."

She chuckled. "Okay."

They arrived at the grill restaurant on the other end of the property facing the gardens. Most of the seating was outdoor, but all the trees shaded them, making it a beautiful, quiet setting for dinner with a gorgeous woman.

She ordered the cedar plank salmon, and he ordered the filet mignon.

While they waited, he asked, "So do you mind showing me your sketches?"

She smiled, pulled her book off the chair beside her, and placed it in front of him.

He pushed away his wineglass and silverware and

opened the cover. He flipped slowly, looking at every page. She'd drawn palm trees, the ocean, a park, a school, a church, a child drawing at a table, so much more. Some were practice pages followed by the finished work. These could be in a gallery.

"These are really good." He glanced over at her.

"I haven't drawn in a while."

Nevertheless, she'd added some great detail. Nic could see her making something of her "hobby" if she wanted to. He flipped to the last page. "Wow." He closed the book and met her gaze. Pride of her bubbled up. "Those were exceptional. Have you thought of selling them? Making a career out of it?"

She blushed and shook her head. "No, I don't think so. I'm not that good."

"Well, I think you are. I bet these would sell. Regardless, you should be proud of yourself." He lifted her hand off the table and kissed the back.

"Thank you."

Their meals arrived, and not a moment too soon. Nic had an appetite—for food and for Cat. He couldn't wait to be alone with her.

As the waiter cleared the plates, he asked, "Would you like some dessert?"

"No, thanks." Cat had no interest in dessert when she was still glowing from Nicholas's comments. She was ridiculously pleased with his praise. Jack had never shown her such interest or appreciation. "Instead of strolling along the beach tonight, want to walk the property?"

"Um, sure. I haven't seen much of the property. I mostly stay on the ocean side." His grin pulled into a boyish smile she was quickly coming to love.

Cat directed them out the back gate to the garden paths, and he wove his fingers in between hers. She watched him take in the scene—the beautiful flowers, the low lighting along the path, the palm trees slowly swaying in the wind.

They reached the second pool and hot tub and paused to admire the view. The gardens were mostly bare of visitors, unlike her other time here. The darkness made the entire walk feel cozy and intimate. Cat never knew how much she loved the outdoors until this trip. Austin could be so hot that she avoided being outside unless necessary.

Nicholas scanned the gardens, tipping his head to watch the trees move in the breeze. "It's so quiet. I bet everyone's at the nightclub."

Cat flashed back to the night of her bachelorette party— all her girls at the club. Before finding Jack screwing that girl, they'd had a great time. Singing, dancing, the scavenger hunt. Riley's face popped into her head, how she'd grinned when she'd walked off with her ex-boyfriend.

Could Cat ever do something so bold? Give a guy a blowjob in a public place.

She bit the inside of her cheek, because even as her

body broke out in a cold sweat, she wanted to try it. Could she try it now? With Nicholas?

They came to a bend in the path where a lone bench was surrounded by dense trees. It beckoned her. "Can we sit for a while?"

"Sure."

She kept hold of his hand, but pressed her body close to his and stretched to meet his lips.

He leaned into her kiss, fusing his lips to hers, his tongue mingling with hers.

She loved kissing him. After a few moments, she broke the kiss. She was stalling. Her heart hammered in her chest as she caressed up and down his leg, coming intentionally close to his manhood.

His hand covered hers. "Cat." His head tipped and the corner of his mouth lifted in question.

"I want to try something." She smoothed her lips together.

He pulled his hand away, wordlessly giving his permission.

She glanced one last time to the right and left, and took to her knees before him.

"Whoa," he whispered as he quickly shot a look up and down the path.

He didn't stop her. She worked his pants loose and in no time, he was free. His gorgeous, thick cock ready for her.

With one hand holding down his briefs and the other

circling his length, she stroked him, loving not only the feel of him, but knowing she caused this reaction from him. She leaned down, encompassing his smooth head with her lips. Her tongue poked his slit. Slowly, she slid down, taking as much as she could into her mouth.

He groaned.

She prayed he was able to keep an eye out for anyone who might be rounding the corner.

Her hand worked in concert with her mouth, up and down. Her tongue circled his tip before she went deep again, sucking on the way up.

"Fuck, Cat," he choked out.

She wanted him to explode in her mouth, she wanted him to lose control. Working faster, his hand cupped the nap of her neck. "Cat."

Did she hear something?

She lifted her head and met his gaze.

Wait. What was that smell?

Nicholas wrinkled his nose. "What is that?"

She rose off the ground as he managed to put himself back together. Her stomach turned over. She plugged her nose with her thumb and forefinger when she saw the intruder.

About ten feet away, heading in their direction, was a skunk.

"Oh God!" Her eyes widened as her heartbeat raced.

"Keep calm. We don't want to get sprayed. But Cat it

would be best to head back. Now." He clasped her hand, keeping one eye on the uninvited guest.

They hurried up the path. She glanced back to see the skunk following, but not really chasing them.

"Let's go a little faster," Nicholas murmured.

She was only too happy to comply.

Soon the skunk was out of sight and the smell no longer clung to the air.

They made it to their building and Nicholas held open the door for her. They each took a deep breath and exhaled. He chuckled and soon she was chuckling too.

In about thirty seconds she would likely be discomfited by her actions, but right then, she could only laugh.

As he walked her to her room, he asked, "How about we call it a night so we can get up early and watch the sunrise?"

Her eyes widened. "I love that idea. But I thought you had a flight?"

"I do, but I have time, beautiful. I'll pick you up at five-thirty."

"Great."

"Thanks for tonight." Nicholas leaned down and wrapped his arms around her, kissing her deeply. "Sweet dreams." He turned and headed to the elevators.

She sighed. That night was monumental for Cat. She'd tried something new, and although it hadn't gone exactly right, she'd at least made an effort.

She hadn't been giving Jack much thought these last

few days, but she realized he was missing out on something amazing. That *she* was amazing.

CHAPTER
Thirteen

Rising from bed at five, Cat knew this was one of her and Nicholas's final days together. He'd asked her to walk the beach and watch the sunrise. He had a flight that morning and would be back later that night. She brushed her teeth, slipped on her bikini, and wrapped the sarong around her waist.

A gentle knock sounded—it could only be him.

With her keycard in hand, she greeted Nicholas at the door.

"Good morning, beautiful." He leaned down, cupping her neck, and kissed her like she was the only thing in the world that mattered.

"Good morning. What a wonderful greeting." Joy blossomed from inside. She wanted to savor every second they had left together.

He laced his fingers between hers and led her through the quiet hotel out the back, into the darkness. They had the beach to themselves. A gentle breeze blew, and the waves washed and retreated ashore, creating a lulling melody of relaxation.

"How about we head up that way?" Nicholas pointed to the east.

They walked hand in hand, passing other resorts, without a soul in sight.

"You know, I'm gonna miss you when you're gone." He broke the silence, voicing her exact thoughts.

"Me too." She glanced up at him. "I've learned so much from you. I'll never forget this time."

A light breeze ruffled his hair, and the corners of his lips curled. "Me either."

She couldn't dwell on not seeing Nicholas again. She'd grown accustomed to having him around during her beach vacation. These last two weeks had been spectacular and Nicholas had played a large role. When she thought about leaving, she ached inside. Instead of being thankful for not mourning the loss and ruminating over Jack, she worried what life would be like in Austin without Nicholas.

They walked several more minutes, getting glimpses of deep pink in the horizon.

They came to the last resort in the row. She could barely make out the small residential houses lining a less-manicured beachfront.

He stopped them at the last wooden cabana structure set for hotel guests to take a break from the sun. "I don't think we should go any farther."

"I agree." She pivoted to return the other way, when he held her wrist. She looked up at him in question.

"Cat, my Careful Cat, I want to try one thing, out here with you."

Her breath caught in her throat. He wouldn't. He wouldn't make love to her out here, when in about fifteen minutes the sun would be on full blaze in the sky.

"Don't worry." He slipped off his T-shirt, leaving only his swim trunks. "I'll be the naked one." His erection tented his shorts.

She looked left and right. "Um, what did you have in mind?"

"Last night, you were giving me the most wonderful blow job... that we didn't get to finish." He reached for the string at his waistband. "Do you think we could finish that now?"

She swallowed hard. Somehow, doing this last night felt different, safer, hidden in the lush greenery of the gardens.

Nicholas slowly pulled against the string of the shorts, loosening them, and pushed them over his hips, letting them fall to the sand. He stepped out of the fabric. Taking her hand, he moved to lean against the cabana post, his back to the direction they'd just come from.

He stood completely naked, tanned skin and ridged muscles on display for her.

Moisture began to dampen her bikini bottoms.

His deep dark blue eyes met hers. "Would you put your

mouth on me, baby?"

She looked over his shoulder—the coast was still clear. Cat lowered herself, her knees sinking into the sand, skimming her fingertips along his stomach and wrapping around his hard length. Without another care about privacy, she took the head of his cock into her mouth.

He groaned as he fingered her hair, gently gripping her head. "Perfect. Oh God, so fucking good. I dreamt of this last night."

She worked his length up and down, licking and sucking on the way up.

"God, Cat. I can't get enough of you. It won't be long, baby."

She tasted his pre-cum, the sweet-salty flavor making her mouth water more and her pussy ache.

He panted and pulled out. "Cat."

She raised her head to meet his eyes. Why had he stopped her? Not another skunk!

"Let me come on your breasts."

Oh, geez. That sounded hot. *And* scary as hell.

His hand reached to the back of her neck at the bow of her bikini top.

Her heart skipped a beat and her eyes darted around him.

"It's okay. No one's around. Please let me come on your breasts. You can keep it on you all day, and smell me while I'm gone. Feel me with you all day."

A gush of liquid oozed onto her nether lips. This might be the hottest, most erotic thing she'd ever done. She was proving to herself she could be more adventurous...

He pulled loose the tie at her neck, and the bathing suit top flopped down, exposing her breasts.

"Gorgeous." He held his cock for her.

She looked one last time at him, then down at his raging erection. She opened her mouth and swallowed him, going back as far as she could handle.

"Yesss, baby," he hissed. His hips flexed, and true to his word, it didn't take long. He pulled out, and with his cock in hand, aimed for her chest.

She watched as the ejaculate squirted, shooting directly on her chest and the top of each breast.

"Take your hands, baby. Rub it in," he said between gasps.

She held his gaze as her hands spread the warm liquid over her breasts, making circles, caressing them as he would.

"Fuck, baby." He grabbed her upper arms, hauling her to standing, and crashed his lips to hers. He kissed her with a commanding finesse, and she met him with equal vigor.

She wanted anything Nicholas would give her. She wanted all of it. Including rubbing his come over her breasts. The rush of passion rolling off when she did that was empowering.

How had she gotten here?

He scattered hot, moist, open-mouthed kisses down

her throat and along her collarbone, then latched on to each pointed nipple, sucking hard.

She whimpered.

He broke the kiss and spun her body against the post he'd been leaning on.

She could start to make out the houses in the distance as the sun rose—the third even had a light on.

Nicholas's hand skimmed down her belly and over her bathing suit bottom. "Baby, I know you want to come, don't you?"

Oh God, he would do this here?

Nicholas didn't wait for her reply. "How about you reach your hands up and grip the post?" He took one wrist and induced her to lift her arms.

In this position, she looked like a seductive mermaid—bare on top, covered on bottom. And he wanted more.

He hadn't planned to do anything illicit—he'd merely wanted to spend time with her on their second-to-last morning together. When the idea came to him of getting her naked in the dark, he couldn't tamp it down. This might be one of his last opportunities to bring her out of her shell.

He slipped a hand under the scarf wrapped around her waist to her pussy. Tunneling under her bikini bottoms, she was soaking. He pushed through her slick channel, loving the mewls spilling from her mouth.

He retrieved his finger. She watched him intently as he

stuck that finger into his mouth, sucking her essence clean off.

Her mouth gaped.

"Baby, I'm going to make you come with my mouth. I'll take off your bikini bottoms. Okay?"

"But the sun—"

"We have time, and you'll still have your wrap on."

He paused, watching her reconcile what he'd asked. He slowly knelt before her and reached under her wrap for her bikini bottoms. He dragged them down her legs, waiting for her objection. It never came. Her grass-green eyes were full of desire.

She stepped out of the garment.

"Legs apart, baby."

As she did, he didn't waste a moment. He dove his tongue into her pussy, lapping at her sweet, musky cream.

She whimpered and squirmed slightly against his face.

He continued tongue-fucking her, giving her as much pleasure as she'd given him.

It was when he lifted the wrap out of the way that he noticed a worker yards away, wiping and organizing the chaise lounges. Nic couldn't be sure if he'd noticed them.

The man would have a rear view of Cat, that was all. There was no way she could see him. Nic decided that he wouldn't stop until she came on his tongue.

He glanced up to see his beautiful woman—eyes closed, mouth slightly open, hands clutching the pole over her head.

His tongue toyed with her swollen clit and she moaned, caught up in the heat of the moment. She'd be coming soon.

The worker looked their way. The man knew what was happening, even in the low light setting. He worked slower, moving chaises, and glancing over occasionally to get a peek.

Nic drove a finger into Cat's dripping pussy and twisted and turned.

Cat whimpered.

With his free hand, he reached for the knot at her wrap.

Her eyes flew open and she dropped her head to see.

"Baby, you're close, but you don't need this on to come. Do you?"

Her eyes went round as saucers.

"Let me get this out of the way." He worked the knot free, letting the fabric fall open. He pulled it down, and not giving her a moment to object, he drove in another finger and claimed her clit with his tongue.

She muffled her shriek and pinched her eyes closed.

The worker stopped what he was doing completely, not even hiding the fact that he was watching them.

The beginning flex of Cat's muscles pulled on Nic's fingers. He worked her harder, feeling the spasms of her clit under this tongue. He loved feeling her come.

He couldn't believe he'd gotten Cat naked out here as the sun rose before her, cascading light over her gorgeous, tanned skin.

When he was sure she was done, he rose, looped his

arm around her, and crushed his naked body to hers. "You are magnificent." He kissed her deeply, greedily.

Her arms wrapped around his neck, coming impossibly closer, kissing him with equal urgency.

Would he ever find another woman who kissed him like Cat did?

He broke the kiss and quickly grabbed her scarf to wrap around her, squatting before her to help with her bikini bottoms.

Nic pulled his shorts on and noticed the worker had gone.

After they were dressed, he smiled, and took her hand. They strolled back to the resort with the bright sun behind them, waking the world to another amazing day.

She lifted her face, still flushed from her hot climax. "I can't believe you made me do that."

He winked. "I didn't make you do anything, sweetheart."

She snorted. "I beg to disagree." Her words betrayed the subtle smile when she tipped her head down. "And someone could have seen us."

Ah, that.

"Wouldn't it be exciting to think someone *could* have seen us? That someone watched us?"

Her head jerked up. "No. Yes. I don't know," she protested.

They stopped. He leaned down, kissed her neck, and

whispered, "Think about it. What if someone, maybe a worker getting ready for the day, saw you take me into your mouth? Saw you rub my come into your succulent breasts? Or saw your naked body writhe as I made you come with my mouth?"

Her breath fluttered over his ear. "Oh, God. Someone saw us, didn't they?"

He straightened to stare into her eyes. "Would you be mad if they did? Be honest."

She watched as her throat worked a swallow. "I guess not," she said meekly.

"I'm sorry. I couldn't hear you."

Her face blushed a brilliant red, the brightest he'd witnessed from this innocent, sensual being.

"I said I guess not."

"You guess not?"

Her lips mushed together. "No, I wouldn't be mad."

"To know someone witnessed me between your open legs? Licking and fucking you with my tongue? Our naked bodies in the daylight?" He paused a beat. "I think that's hot."

She stared at him and straightened her posture. "Nicholas, that was the hottest thing I've ever done. And yes, knowing someone watched us makes it even hotter."

He squeezed her hand. "That's right, my Careful Cat. Hot as Hades."

She gave him a sheepish smile. "Maybe not 'Careful'

anymore."

He flashed his pearly whites and shook his head slowly. "Uh-uh. More like Confident Cat. Or better still, Craving Cat."

She chuckled, her whole face transformed from the timid woman he'd met eleven days ago. He loved to see her happy.

How long would it take to get over her? He feared he was in too deep.

CHAPTER
Fourteen

Cat arrived at the restaurant early to soak up her last day of vacation and wait for Nicholas. He'd said he had a morning appointment he couldn't change, but would meet her for brunch after he landed. He'd cleared the day to be with her.

The following day, she'd be gone.

She sipped on her coffee, trying to push that thought out of her head.

A man at the threshold sauntered into view. She knew that form. *It couldn't be.*

Jack.

No, no, no, no, no, no, no.

He smiled as he crossed the carpeted floor toward her table by the window. "Hello, Cat. You look fabulous."

He was the last person she'd expected to see. "Jack, what are you doing here?"

He pulled the only other chair at the table close to her and sat. "I came to see you."

"I can see that."

He leaned forward and clasped her hand. "I wanted to give you space. I'm sorry. I know I screwed up, but I'll spend the rest of my life making it up to you. If you give me that chance."

"Whoa." Her fingers pressed against her lips.

At that moment, the waitress arrived. "Can I get you something to drink, sir?"

"Coffee, please," he replied. He looked back at Cat. "Have you ordered? I'm starving."

"Well, actually—" She glanced toward the door. She wanted to eat with Nicholas, but she wasn't prepared to tell Jack that she'd met someone. Regardless of how temporary their relationship was, if Jack knew about Nicholas, he would lose his crap. Cat *definitely* didn't want to have that conversation right then.

"You go ahead and order," she told him.

"Eggs benedict with whole wheat toast and crispy bacon."

The waitress nodded and retreated.

"Look, I asked about extending our time here—"

"Our time?"

He exhaled. "I mean, I can have my own room, but Cat, let's take a few days and talk, reconnect."

Shit! This was her vacation, *not* their honeymoon.

Leave it to Jack to ruin something meaningful to her, once again.

He sincerely appeared remorseful, but geez! She didn't want to be a bitch, she just didn't want him here. She didn't want to talk to him. She never wanted to talk about that fateful night.

Tears gathered in her eyes. Clearly the pain was still raw.

Nicholas came into view at the coffee bar. He glanced at her, then down at his coffee.

"Jack, I'll be right back."

Nicholas could tell by the pasty, white skin that the man crouched beside Cat, holding her hand, was her ex.

Her gaze locked on him as she crossed the room.

"Hi."

"Hi. Look, I'm sorry, but—"

"Your ex showed up. I can see that."

Her beautiful face filled with so much emotion. "I'm sorry. I'll try and get rid of him."

She had to be tormented by Jack's unexpected appearance. Nicholas wouldn't make this situation any harder for her.

He clasped her hand, sure that Jack couldn't see, not that Nicholas cared too much. "Don't worry about it. Talk to him. You need to get closure. It's okay."

Her eyes looked glassy.

He wanted to tear the other man apart for ruining their last day. But what could he do? Nicholas stayed kind and congenial. He didn't know their full past together. Cat needed support right now, not a jealous—what?—lover. Nic had no claim to her.

He held her gaze. "Remember everything you've learned these past two weeks. You're a new woman, Cat. A confident woman." He kissed the back of her hand. "I want to kiss you goodbye, but he's watching." He gave her a small smile.

Her eyebrows pulled together, but he couldn't stay. "Good luck to you." He lifted his coffee and walked out of the restaurant.

He resisted with every ounce of his will power not to look back at her. If Jack was watching, at least now the interaction could be explained away easily enough. Especially if she decided not to reveal everything to the undeserving bastard.

Put a smile on your face, Cat, and get back in there. If it's meant to be, you can find a way to forgive him.

Although, geezus, Nic didn't want her to ever see that piece of shit again. But he didn't exactly have anything to offer her instead. They lived a thousand miles apart. He had his career, and she had hers.

Coffee cup in hand, he slipped on his sunglasses and walked the patio, making his way to the beach.

He considered ordering breakfast, but really had no appetite. He slipped off his shoes and socks and left them on the chaise lounge, walking aimlessly along the surf.

The ache inside was the exact feeling he'd had when his

best friend had died. Dillon had been so full of life. He'd died in a freak accident a few years prior, teaching Nicholas the most important lesson of all. Live life to the fullest.

Dillon had done that, and Nicholas had sworn he'd do the same thing.

Now, however, there was no zest for life, only a chasm of emptiness.

He knew his time with Cat had to end. Of course. But at least they could have had one last day, and night, together. But that was shot to hell because of her ex.

He wanted to hit something.

He didn't even get to fucking kiss her goodbye.

Cat.

Cat's head pounded, and pressing her fingers into the ache didn't do a hill of beans good.

When Jack had shown up at the resort, Cat had wanted to cry. Truly, how could he have ruined her last full day on the island? Her last day with Nicholas.

The strangest sensation fell over her as she watched and listened to Jack. She couldn't believe she'd almost married him. She'd half-expected for some rush of emotion to hit her when he'd taken her hand, given her a heartfelt apology, and begged her to think about trying to reconcile.

But it hadn't.

In fact, she felt nothing but pity for him. She refrained from telling him as much.

They'd walked outside and found a shady table to talk. About an hour into the conversation, it was pretty clear she was playing therapist, something she'd sworn she'd never do for any man. As giving as she was, she knew better...but it didn't matter too much. She would likely never see Jack again.

After hours of talking, she closed the door of the taxi cab behind him, finally waving him off. He'd wanted to fly back with her in the morning, but Cat stood her ground and told him to leave immediately. It took some convincing, but thankfully he'd agreed and was on his way to the airport.

She had successfully exorcised the demon of a broken engagement by a cheating fiancé.

All she had left to do was try and salvage her remaining precious moments with Nicholas.

CHAPTER
Fifteen

Nic heard a knock at his hotel door. His heart skipped a beat.

He glanced at the time—six-thirty at night. He set his drink down and crossed the room.

The day had been shit, frankly. He'd barely eaten. All he could think about was Cat, and a few times Cat and the asshole. He hoped she'd found the guts to tell him to take a long walk off a short pier.

But he also knew there was a chance she'd take him back, and Nic would never see her again.

He opened the door. Standing before him in the same pink dress as earlier, Cat gave him a tentative smile.

"I told Jack we're through. He's on a flight back to Austin."

Excellent. Nic paused, thinking about his next move. "Come in."

She strode to the middle of the room and pivoted to face him. She looked adorable—bright eyes focused on him, waiting to see what he'd do.

He stalked closer—his heart damn-near beat out of his chest.

He stopped two feet in front of her. Maybe it was the alcohol talking, but he needed to say the words. "I can't give you forever."

She didn't bat an eye. "I know. I want right now."

Fuck! That's all he wanted, all he could ask for. Well, maybe one more thing.

"Did you eat?"

"Some. I'm not hungry for food." She made two steps in his direction, laying a hand on his chest.

They had a few hours left together. He would make them count. He still didn't move and knew it was likely making her insane that he hadn't touched her yet. "Cat, I want you to spend the night here, with me. But if you do, know that until you need to leave for the airport, you're mine. Anything I say. Can you live with that?"

She swallowed, but kept his gaze. "Yes," she answered in a small voice though her eyes sparkled.

Fuck! He wanted her, in so many ways, every way. His dick strained against his jeans.

He snaked an arm around her and hauled her body against his. His lips crashed to hers and consumed her mouth. Her precious, warm mouth.

Her arms circled around his neck causing her wonderful breasts to compress against his chest.

He broke the kiss. "What are you wearing under this dress?"

"Nothing."

Double fuck! Just as he suspected. *I'm going to fucking consume every inch of you.*

He stepped back and whipped off his T-shirt. Her fingertips slid down his chest to his abs, skirting the waistband of his jeans. He'd love nothing more than to feel her mouth encompassing his dick, but he needed her naked for him. Now.

Pulling her closer, he skimmed his free hand over her thigh and under her dress. Her bare hip broke out in goosebumps as he caressed her silky skin.

"Nicki," she pleaded.

His finger skated through her slit, her soaking wet slit. Damn, he wanted to haul her up against the closest wall and ram into her with the force of a tornado. Maybe later. For now, he had a different plan. A plan to stretch her boundaries to a place she'd never imagine going in a million years. He knew he could convince her of anything, she was so hot to have whatever he might give her.

His lips fused to hers and he walked her backward to the bed. He broke their kiss. "Sit."

She sat on the edge of the bed and waited for him.

He pulled open the top drawer of the dresser to retrieve a tie. He rarely needed to wear one for business, but he'd learned early on to pack one or two every trip, just in case.

She tracked his movements.

Without saying a word, he lifted the tie before her eyes and tied it snuggly at the back of her head like a blindfold. "Don't move," was his only command.

He eyed the round table in front of the wall of windows leading to the balcony. He pushed open the sliding glass door completely. *This'll be tight.*

He dragged the table out to the balcony, planting it just short of the railing to give him room to maneuver about.

Walking back inside, Cat sat right where he'd left her, her mouth slightly agape and the pulse on her neck fluttering gently. She could likely feel the warm air coming in from outside and was no doubt wondering if he had plans for them on the balcony.

He knelt before her, laying kisses over her lips, her neck, and her shoulders.

Her breath was coming in shallow pants.

He rose, grasping her hand, and brought her to a standing position. "Wrap your legs around me."

He hoisted her up into his arms, his hands gripping her gorgeous globes bare beneath the fabric of her dress.

Her lips found his as she held him tight. Her kisses were intoxicating.

Carrying her to the balcony, he positioned her, facing the ocean, and set her on the table.

"Oh God," she breathed.

"Shh." He knew she was nervous, but this was his

chance to break down her protective walls, and he'd happily take it. In the small space between the table and railing, he knelt before her. "My sweet Cat, my courageous Cat." He stroked her thighs up and down, pushing them apart. "You are mine tonight. You know that, right?"

"Yes." She licked her lips.

He slid her dress a few inches higher up her legs. "Can you feel the breeze off the ocean when it hits your pussy?"

She swallowed. "Yes."

"Good. Give me your hand."

She hesitated a fraction of a second, but gave it to him.

He placed her hand high on her thigh, a slight hint of her nether lips coming into view. "You're going to touch yourself for me."

She whimpered.

"Shh. You can do this. I want this. I want you to feel good, but this will also make me feel good. You've come so far. Do this for you. Do this for me."

Sunlight remained in the sky. They probably had another hour and twenty minutes before evening.

Her fingertip inched closer and pulled up the center of her wet slit. She moaned.

His dick surged. He opened his button and fly to give his dick a break from the pain caused by constriction.

Gently, he moved her dress higher, wanting a full view of her masturbating.

"Nicki."

He crashed his lips over hers, quieting her protest. Nic's room was high up in the resort, one floor above hers. Only if someone specifically looked up and squinted hard would they be able to see Cat.

"My pussy," he breathed over her lips. "Don't stop."

Taking one leg, caressing it, he slowly brought it to the side and set it on the top of the railing.

She didn't make a sound. *Good girl.*

He did the same thing to her other leg, effectively spreading her legs open in a V with him between.

Blowing a small breath over her burgeoning clit, he said, "Now, don't stop playing with this beautiful pink pussy and lay all the way back."

Her head might hang off the edge of the table, but he wouldn't keep her in that position for long.

She lay back, her legs and pussy bare for his viewing. *Almost there.*

"Are you close to coming?"

She panted. "Yes."

"Good. I want you to come." He drove one then two fingers inside her slippery wet pussy and watched as she squirmed on the table, moaning low. She rode out the waves of her glorious climax.

Before she had a chance to move, he slid the dress higher, to just below her tits, and pinned her hands to the table while he licked her feverishly.

She called out, but quickly clamped her lips closed.

He ate her, savoring her quiet mewls and how her legs quivered when he brought her to the edge and pulled back.

"Don't move."

He reached into his back pocket and sheathed himself with a rubber. He caught a glimpse of movement two balconies over. An audience.

Laying kisses over Cat's inner thigh, he saw the neighbor wave to someone in the room. A female joined him, her jaw dropping at the scene before them. Their audience smiled.

Nic's kisses traveled up Cat's body, pushing against the fabric to expose her delicious breasts. He sucked and laved her nipples. Then, he whispered, "Arms up."

Cat paused, but he waited. Finally, she raised her arms above her head, her palms coming in contact with the glass door.

He slid her dress off her body and let if fall to the floor. Her smokin' body, ripe nipples, and bare pussy completely on display for him, and their audience, who was now kissing and fondling each other while watching Nic and Cat.

"Keep your arms there."

He crouched down again to feast on her. She tasted divine. He would miss this when she was gone.

With his hands under her ass cheeks, he brought her closer to his mouth, forcing her legs to widen.

Nic glanced at the couple two doors down to see the man had lifted the woman's swim cover-up and was fucking her from behind.

Nic would remember this scene for the rest of his life. How Cat had brought so much joy and inspiration, a fantasy come to life. He hoped she'd leave feeling the same way about him.

Sweat dripped down the back of his neck.

"Nicki," she begged.

"Do you want me to make you come?"

"Yes," she replied softly.

"I can't hear you."

"Yes," she said louder.

He slammed two fingers into her pussy while simultaneously sucking on her hard, eager clit. She cried out before covering her mouth.

He pushed and pulled his fingers, sucking and laving every inch of her pussy. It took only a few seconds for another orgasm to rip through her, squirting on him in the process.

He gave her a moment to savor it before he stood and dove into her, slamming clear to the end, over and over, allowing his release to overtake him.

Realizing she was coming again, as her muscles squeezed him tight, he sucked on a nipple, adding to her crest.

He collapsed over her, panting into her neck. Her arms and legs came around him.

"You were positively incredible. I'm so proud of you."

He pushed off her blindfold.

She blinked. "Someone could have seen us."

He debated his next move and opted for complete disclosure. "Someone did."

She tensed. All over.

"In fact, it was *someones*. A couple saw us from their balcony. They saw you spread out for me to feast, then enter you."

Her pussy muscles contracted around him. Her mouth hung open.

"They were so turned on, they fucked while watching us."

She gasped. "They did?"

He motioned to the right, and she turned to see the couple as they walked back inside, arm in arm.

"Ohmigod."

Nic's erection, never fully deflated, flexed back to life. He pushed into her gently. "You looked so hot."

"I can't believe it," she whispered.

He kept rocking her on the table, loving that she didn't make him stop to go back inside.

"A couple enjoying one another is a beautiful thing." He leaned down, kissing and nibbling her plump lips. "I will never forget this night. This trip. I will never forget you, Cat."

She squeezed him tighter and kissed his neck. "I won't forget you either."

His thrusts picked up pace. He should have changed his

condom, but he didn't want to stop. He kissed her deeply, owning her mouth, memorizing every inch of it.

With her body wrapped around his, he rocked them to another climax. If only he could make this night last forever.

Last night had gone better than anything Cat could have ever imagined.

Her body ached at the memory of Nicholas. Her body was trained to crave his. She'd been beyond nervous when she'd approached his hotel room door.

Ha! Then he'd taken her outside and set her on a table. Nervous didn't even being to describe how she'd felt.

She'd shoved down her apprehension since it was their last night—literally, hours left—she wasn't about to ruin their time together. Deep inside, she trusted him.

Unbelievably, the higher he had her climb, the further he'd pushed her, the less inhibited she'd become. Blindfolding her? He'd known exactly what he was doing.

And knowing a couple had watched them... It was simply the most erotic thing she'd ever done. Probably ever would do.

She seemed to be saying that a lot on this trip.

Nicholas had kept her up most of the night. He fed her, bathed her, and made love to her twice more. Now, as the sun illuminated his hotel room, he gently laid her on her back, stroking and kissing her body, despite the sleepiness that still clouded her brain.

She sighed as his tongue trailed over her nipple, the sheet moving to the side to reveal both breasts.

"Good morning, my sweet Cat."

She moaned her reply as his caresses and kisses traveled south.

Slowly he pushed her legs apart, placing kisses at the apex of her thighs, making her wake up in the most pleasant fashion. He gently inserted a finger as he laved her excited clit.

Several more strokes and she panted as he pushed in a second finger. "Mmm."

"God, Cat. You always get so wet."

He stopped and rose.

"Oh, don't stop." Her climax lingered so close to the surface.

For the first time, she opened her eyes to see his lust-filled gaze on her. He grinned. "I need to be inside you. But as much as I'd love nothing more than to come inside you, have you take some of me with you, I need to get a condom." He reached for the nightstand, and she cupped his forearm.

He looked down at her, questioning.

"We may not need that. Are you clean?"

His brows pulled together. "Yes. My company requires annual physicals. I was tested two months ago."

"Nicki, I'm on the pill. It never seemed to matter to Jack. He insisted on condoms. Maybe he was protecting me." She shrugged. "But I'm okay without a condom, if you are."

Passion flushed his cheeks. "Oh, fuck, Cat." He crashed his lips over hers, a hand cupping the back of her neck, taking what he wanted.

He lay down, his hips aligned with hers, his naked cock at her entrance.

"Oh, God. Nicki, please. I don't think I can wait another second." She looped her arms and legs around him.

His arm wrapped around her waist, one hand brushed a stray hair from her face. "Are you sure?"

"Very."

Slowly, he slid into her channel, pushed against her walls, creating the most delicious sensation.

She panted, his eyes trained on hers as he claimed more room inside her. Finally, he pinned her clear to her end. He growled.

"You feel so damn good, Cat. Thank you for this, baby. For everything you gave to me during this trip." He thrust, driving head-on to some deep spot of sensation Cat had never felt before.

"Oh."

Nicki did it again and again, short thrusts slamming into the end of her. She straddled a fine line between pleasure and pain.

Her breath came faster, as did his. She squirmed and a trickle of sweat slid down her neck.

His gaze was glued to hers, his muscles working to hold her securely as he powered and penetrated her so deeply.

"Nicki. Oh."

"Let it go, my beautiful Cat."

She was delirious with sensation, building, building. Finally the floodgates opened and her orgasm exploded with such force she almost passed out.

Nicki covered her mouth with his, driving his tongue into her body as he did his cock. In several short thrusts, he shot his seed deep inside her. A first for her.

He collapsed to her side, breathing heavily into the crux of her neck.

After a few moments, he lifted his head to meet her eyes. "That was fucking amazing. Now, there is a little piece of me you can take with you."

She sighed at the truth *and* the absurdity of it. But deep inside, she loved having this connection with him.

"Seriously Cat, you're beautiful. You're wonderful. These two weeks have been the best in my life. I'm so glad you got closure with your ex, but selfishly, I'm glad we met and got to spend time together. It's been great getting to know you."

She smiled back at him, a bittersweet smile. "You too."

This is the beginning of goodbye.

CHAPTER
Sixteen

Cat was depleted on so many levels.

She stared out the window from her first class seat, a bittersweet emotion filling her to the brim. The last few hours with Nicholas had been amazing. He cherished her, used her body, took as much as he gave. Cat was emotionally and physically drained.

And the way she'd nearly cried a dozen times, she knew, she'd fallen in love with him.

Nicholas had gone with her to the airport, kissing her one last time, with a promise to each other they'd try and stay connected. But living a thousand miles apart, plus traveling so much for work, wasn't exactly conducive to a relationship. They both understood that this was a vacation fling that had little hope of a future.

She dozed a few times during the flight, but mostly the past two weeks played over in her mind like a favorite song she knew every word to. She replayed every touch, every kiss, every orgasm. The sex she and Nicholas had was out of this world good, and crazy risky at times.

Geez! She was crazy to do some of the things she'd done. What would she tell Celeste? Unbidden, she chuckled softly. *Celeste won't believe most of what I did.*

When she landed, she dragged her luggage through customs and out to a cab. She shot off a text to Cel, telling her she'd arrived and needed sleep. Then she shot off a text to Nicholas.

I've landed. Someone kept me up all night, so I'm going to bed soon. :)

He replied almost immediately.

I'm glad you arrived safely. My night was equally spectacular. I miss you already. Sleep well.

She smiled at the text, trying not to let the unshed tears break free. She missed him too. Of course. But she couldn't let the thoughts of him consume her. Those two weeks were probably the best of her life. And now it was time to move on. Pack away her lovely, steamy memories of a man who'd brought her out of her shell, who'd showed her an adventurous side of sex, who'd showed her she could move on from the hurt from Jack and not just survive, but thrive.

Cat had no regrets. What Nicholas had given her she would treasure forever. She *was* a beautiful woman with a lot to give. She didn't need a man to make her feel that way, but when the time came, she would be strong enough to recognize a real, caring man, and she had no doubt she would find love again.

She'd pick herself up by Monday morning, and pour her energy into work. But that night, as she walked through her apartment door, dropped her luggage, stripped out of her clothes, and crawled into bed, she cried herself to sleep. The tears fell, drenching her pillow.

How could someone survive having their heart broken twice in the same month?

Nic walked into the Orlando office, a week after his trip to the Caribbean, two weeks after Cat had returned home. Every time he thought of her, he wanted to smile at all the incredible memories, but there was something else. Something more melancholy that really shouldn't be there.

What they'd shared was out of this world, spectacular. He'd do it all again in a heartbeat. Specifically, he'd do it all again with *her*.

He'd had sex with women—on the beach, or otherwise outside. Thrilling, fucking hot sex. So why did the experience with Cat feel so damn different? Was it because she was no longer around? He had no one to see and talk to after a busy day and he'd enjoyed their companionship.

Juliette Maker, his boss's boss, rang his line, bringing him back to the present. He had a job to do. Success was just a hairsbreadth away.

He sat straight in his chair and pulled closer to his desk scattered with so much paper one might not know it was brown.

"Hey, Nic. You tore it up this last trip."

"Thanks."

"Damn. You got Wilson practically drooling."

Randall Wilson was the company's CEO. He was just as driven as Nic. Nic had told him in so many words that one day he'd have *his* job. Credit to Wilson, he'd said *Then, one day you will.*

That had been the best fucking day of his life, until he'd met Cat.

"Well, good. Tourism is amping back up down there."

"Bullcrap tourism. It's you. Now I just need to figure out how to replicate you. Let's go out to lunch this week. You open Thursday?"

What? "Yes."

"Great. See you then."

What did she mean "replicate"? *She better not be trying to divide up my territory.*

Nic hung up the phone and stared out the window. It was a bright sunny day. Cat's sleepy smile the morning she'd left popped in his head. The way she pinched her eyes closed at the light, the way she sighed when he kissed her belly, the way she moaned when he slid inside her warm wet pussy.

He reached for his cell phone, thinking about texting her.

MIA LONDON

No. He couldn't, he had a ton of work to catch up on. Besides she probably didn't want to be bothered by some fling she had on vacation.

She'd want to move on with her life. Find her forever guy. Nic thought of her ex.

Shit! She better not get back together with that dirt bag.

Nic clenched his fist. If that guy tried to weasel his way back into her life, he would fucking level him.

Focus, Nic. That is not your problem.

He spun back to his laptop and plugged in the numbers for next month's sales forecast.

Cat opened the container of crispy shredded beef in chili sauce, questioning if she was even hungry.

Celeste set her lemon chicken on the coffee table. She strode to the kitchen and returned with a bottle of sauvignon blanc and two glasses. After pouring, she settled into the cushy armchair and eyed Cat. "You seem down. Still thinking about Nicholas?"

Cat shrugged a shoulder. "It's weird. He was just a rebound guy, but it's almost like it hurts worse than my breakup with Jack."

Cel nodded thoughtfully. "Do you regret it? Do you regret going?"

Cel would probably blame herself, if she wasn't already,

177

for Cat's broken heart. "No. No way."

She wouldn't trade those two weeks for anything. The experience had made her stronger and wiser, opening her eyes to the sensuality of human nature. She was proud of herself for taking risks and stepping out of her safe boundaries. She didn't know what the future held, but she was forever changed, thanks to Nicholas. She was more likely to take a risk and savor some of the thrill that life had to offer. Nicholas had showed her another side.

"I'm just floored at my response after such a short time being together. How could I have fallen in love with him? It's been a few weeks and my feelings aren't fading. Is there such a thing as getting over a rebound guy?"

Cel shook her head. "I don't think there's a standard answer for that. Everyone is different. Cat, you may have to face the possibility that you *have* fallen in love with him, and it's real. So if you can't be with him, hold yourself together, and do what you can to take it one day at a time."

She dipped her head and poked the fork around in her takeout container. Sounds easier than it really is, she thought.

Thursday afternoon, Nic met Juliette in the lobby of their high-rise office building. She motioned with an index finger while she wrapped up a phone call.

Juliette was a driver. She'd worked her way to VP of

Sales through a history of strategic positions with mostly Fortune 500 companies. Once, she'd been asked to interview with a company while she was eight months pregnant. They made her an offer that day and told her they'd wait until she'd completed her maternity leave. *Wow*. She was now a fifty-five-year-old smart, tenacious, bulldog in heels. Nic admired her for all she'd accomplished and how she'd done it. He could learn a lot from her.

"Sorry about that. Let's head down to Russell's. I've got us reservations."

Russell's was an upscale steak and seafood restaurant, a Zagat top choice, and a local favorite known for their fresh seafood and prime beef selections. Most people who dined there during the day were on an expense account.

Juliette sat and, after ordering ice water, pulled a folder from her large handbag. "So Nic, your numbers are excellent. The territory is the fastest growing in the company, and on target to be the most profitable, if it keeps going the way it is."

"Thank you." What more could he say? The fact that she was singling him out for a meeting like this, *not* in her office, and his boss, Alan, wasn't there, both excited him and made him nervous.

She looked up from her notes and sat back, eyeing him. "Where do you see yourself in the next few years, Nic?"

He took a sip from his water glass. "In management. I suspect the company will continue on this growth trajectory and may add director-level positons. I could step into that role before VP."

Her grin stretched, eventually showing some straight white teeth, seemingly not fazed by his cockiness. Of course, Juliette had an excellent poker face.

"I figured as much. So, Wilson and I are in agreement— you need to take on a management role sooner, rather than later."

Nic swallowed. Was he hearing that right? They were ready to promote him now? He didn't want to get his hopes up.

"Again, you've done a great job. How do you feel about being the regional manager for the Eastern US Region?"

That was his boss's job.

"Before you wonder, Alan is being promoted to head HR. He's blessed this move and knows that we're speaking today."

Alan had given his blessing, which was exactly what Nic had been hoping for. "Wow."

"As I mentioned on the phone, I need to replicate you." She grinned, likely seeing the confusion on his face. "Having you in charge of a sales team, teaching them, training them to make them as successful as you is where you need to be. As much as we'd love to have you stay in that territory, it makes more sense to create more Nics who can be just as successful in many territories."

He nodded.

She flipped a sheet of paper before him. "The pay structure is a bit different, but there is still a commission component based on how well your team performs against quota."

Wow. The figure was impressive. More than what he was making now, with a focus on a salary instead of commission. Mentally, he calculated his timeline of his salary compared to his brother's and sister's.

"What do you think?"

He raised his head. "Juliette, this is great. I'm happy and surprised." So why didn't it feel right? This was what he'd been wanting for years. "I can't wait to start."

She leaned forward to offer her hand. "You deserve it." They shook and returned to more basic conversation about the company and future projections.

Normally, he'd call his brother and sister—do a little celebrating. But sitting there, all Nic wanted to do was call Cat. He wanted to celebrate with her.

The food was filling, but for some reason, Nic couldn't remember the taste. It was like half of him was present and the other half was someplace else.

CHAPTER
Seventeen

Nic hoisted his oversized duffle bag out of the trunk of the rental car and headed up the path to his parents' house.

The door swung open as he reached for the knob. "You're here," his mother exclaimed, bubbling with happiness as she slung her arms around him.

"Hi, Mom." He dropped his bag to hug her and leaned down to kiss her cheek, inhaling her signature scent. Her hair was cut shorter, but otherwise she hadn't changed a bit in the four months since he'd last seen her.

She stepped back, grinning. "Let's go inside. Everyone's here."

They walked into the kitchen, which was a spacious, well-equipped room with an over-sized island perfect for the amount of food Mom had spread out. People sat on stools to chat with the cook.

Lisa stood beside Dad as he mixed a pitcher of margaritas. Jared, Lisa's husband, was conversing with Samuel and his girlfriend, Monica, also a doctor. Thinking about, Lisa might have right: their relationship seemed to be getting serious. This was Monica's second family event to attend with Samuel.

"Brother, you made it." Samuel offered a hand and leaned in for an off-center hug.

"How's it goin'?" Nic hugged Monica, Jared, his dad, and lastly Lisa—her usual sparkly self seemed to bubble with extra enthusiasm.

"Glad you're here, son. Glad everyone's here." Dad patted him on the back twice.

Mom pulled cheese and some veggies from the fridge while Nic sat on the vacant barstool at the island.

"So, what's new? You seem kinda quiet." Samuel pointed his way with a carrot stick.

Both his siblings were older by a few years. Nic would often be the brunt of their jokes but there were equal times that he knew his brother and sister cared. "Nah, I'm good. Lot on my mind. I was offered the regional manager position last week."

"Aw, sweetie, that's great," Mom said, pleased.

"Good job," Samuel chimed in with the others.

Nic nodded. "Thanks."

"Perfect timing then. Let's all grab a glass for a toast." Dad filled the blue-rimmed margarita glasses, then waited for everyone to join in. "Congrats, Nic. Here's to a great reunion of the Westbrooks and happy Independence Day weekend."

"Here, here," they all called out before taking a sip.

Lisa set down her glass, pushing it toward the center of the island.

"Something wrong, sweetie?" Mom's brow furrowed.

Lisa glanced around a beat. "Since we're making announcements, I have one." She looked over at Jared, who wrapped his arm around her waist. "*We* have one. We're having a baby."

"Aw. Congratulations. That's great." The family members spoke over one another, then Mom, Dad, and Monica took turns giving Lisa hugs.

Nic smiled because she looked happy—so did Jared. Nic was happy too, but also confused. Previously, his sister hadn't shown much interest in having babies, not while she had a successful law practice.

Samuel asked aloud what he'd been thinking. "How will you work that with the practice? Will you hire another attorney?"

Dipping her broccoli in the ranch dip, she replied, "I could, but I'm thinking about selling so I can focus on our family."

Nic's brother and sister were just as driven toward success as he'd always been. Nic stared at Lisa, trying to process what his sister was saying. He'd never expected she'd consider having babies *and* now selling the business? He was dumbfounded.

The conversation continued like Lisa hadn't just

dropped a bomb. Drinking and snacking. Was he the only one that thought this was out of character for her?

After dinner, Nic took his duffle to the downstairs office that had a deep sofa he could sleep on. He didn't mind not having a bed. It would only be for a few days. Besides, his siblings all had significant others with them. If he'd brought Cat, he would have gotten a hotel.

That thought came out of left field and stopped him cold in his tracks.

There wasn't a day that passed since Saint Lucia that he hadn't thought of her. It was driving him nearly insane. He missed her every minute of every day.

"Hey."

He turned to see his brother walking through the doorway. "Hey. What's up?"

"Just checkin' on you. You seemed a little quiet at dinner." Samuel leaned against the desk.

Nic threw his toiletry bag on the sofa. "Isn't it strange that Lis wants to quit and sell her practice to start a family?"

Samuel grimaced and shook his head "Some women know when it's time to have kids, even if they never thought they wanted them before. She is thirty-five. Biologically speaking, she doesn't have time to waste."

Nic nodded. He didn't find satisfaction in the answer. The three of them were competitive, always pushing each other to greatness. He had the throttle at full speed while his sister was backing off.

Just as Samuel walked out Lisa walked in, carrying his limited-edition Nike Air Jordan's. "I think these are yours," she announced with a smile.

"Thanks. Hey, before you go. How are you feeling?"

She laid a hand over her belly, her skin glowing. "I feel good. Doc said things are progressing nicely."

"I didn't think you were interested in having babies."

She shrugged, not seeming to take offense at his personal comment. "I don't think I ever ruled it out, but I guess it just felt right to start now."

He didn't know how to respond. This simply didn't seem like the sister he knew. The one who'd race him to finish dinner, even as Mom scolded them. The one who would go toe-to-toe with her brothers over grades. The one who graduated from college a semester early just so she'd have bragging rights.

"Look, I'm not saying it was an easy decision, but the practice is just work. It's just a job. *This* is family." She rubbed a hand over her belly again. "And Nic, life isn't a competition." She grinned. "We all may be competitive, but it's fun and games. Finding a person you want to spend your life with, building a family, growing together—that's important. That's what matters most." She paused for a second, and he wondered if she would continue but then she kissed his cheek, stroked his forearm, and left without further conversation.

Nic lay on the couch and stared up at the ceiling, replaying the night, his time in the Caribbean, his meeting with Juliette, all of it. He felt like he was on the cusp of something amazing or something incredibly horrific, and he just couldn't put his finger on it.

Growing up, Nic would compete with his brother and sister. Lisa was right: they were all driven and competitive. He would compete with his friends, and not just in sports. He would compete with himself. Having the best and being the best drove him, in everything. Dillon was right there along with him.

But now, after Lisa's announcement, he was forced to stop and reconsider. For some reason, he was internalizing *her* decision. And it shouldn't affect him in the least. So why was it he was wide awake at one in the morning rehashing his entire life?

All he wanted to do was talk to Cat. She was so flippin' easy to talk to. And smart too. They'd traded a few texts, nothing deep. He wanted to plan a trip to see her, but now with his promotion...

If Alan was moving to Human Resources, they'd want someone in the position right away. Nic was the perfect candidate, and everyone knew it.

He pressed his fingers against his temples. Was that what he really wanted?

He chuckled. Once Cat had said *Things aren't always as they seem*, when she'd spoken of her ex-fiancé. Now, Nic was wondering about that himself. Would advancement in his job, his career, somehow prove he was just as successful as his siblings—the doctor and the lawyer? Was that how he was going to measure his success? He'd done it for so long, he never questioned it. Never stopped to think whether that was the best barometer.

If his best friend were alive, he would share everything going on in his life. Dillon had had great insight and already knew Nic was a workaholic; no time for relationships. But knowing Dillon, he might have said *Live life to the fullest, because from where I stand you wouldn't be lying around thinking about her, you'd be with her.*

Nic rolled to his side, shutting his eyes, willing sleep to come.

CHAPTER
Eighteen

The dreaded Saturday had arrived.

"No, the dress is definitely better than the jeans." Celeste pointed from her perch on Cat's bed.

Cat had been trying to get out of this blind date all week. Last week, Bethany and Riley had come over. All four of them had watched a chick flick and ate pizza. Cat still wasn't herself, and her girls knew it. It had only been a month since she'd last seen Nicholas.

"You have to find a way to get over him," Bethany had said with concern and love in her blue eyes.

"I know. This obsession with a rebound guy is starting to affect my job. I forgot an important update on a file I was working on, and I think I missed a meeting this week. Everyone seems to be walking on eggshells around me, thinking I'm broken up about Jack."

They all nodded.

"Well, you know what they say: the fastest way to get over a guy is to get under another." Riley grinned, but damn if Riley didn't believe her own advice.

Cat rolled her eyes.

"She's kinda right, babe. You need to date." Cel tipped her head.

So, here she stood, trying on clothes that would meet Celeste's approval for a date that they'd arranged with a guy named Stefano.

What the hell was she thinking? Seriously.

"Okay, perfect. Wear your navy heels and don't forget the flower. You've got fifteen minutes before your Uber arrives," Cel called out as she left her bedroom.

Fifteen minutes left. Fifteen minutes to think of a good excuse to get out of this thing.

Oh whatever. Maybe if I go on this date, they'll leave me alone for a while.

She walked into the kitchen with a minute to spare and received the Celeste Beckworth nod of approval. "Look, I'm probably gonna crash at Nate's tonight. He has a gig on Sixth Street and asked me to hang with him afterward," she said as she waggled her brows, her eyes twinkling.

"Okay. I guess I can wait until tomorrow to give you all the gory details," Cat replied on a sigh and headed out the front door.

The driver pulled up to Andiamo's Italian Bar and Grill, and the valet opened her car door. Cat had been to the restaurant a few times with Jack. The place served some excellent eggplant parm and tiramisu. *At least there's that.*

Even as she tried not to slump in her chair, Cat couldn't stop thinking that she'd rather be somewhere else— anywhere else—besides on a date. She had only one person on her mind these days—Nicholas Westbrook.

She'd tried telling herself it was just sex, but after a hundred times, that lie simply didn't stick. She'd even researched paralegal jobs in Orlando—a few looked enticing, but she wasn't about to push herself on the man. If they were meant to be together, wouldn't he have just asked her, *Hey, have you ever thought of living in Orlando?*

They'd hardly texted each other, as he was likely moving on. She clearly felt more for him than he did for her, and that was her deciding factor. She didn't apply to any of the jobs in Orlando and scolded herself for not being over him already.

Her eyes began to water. She quickly lifted her cloth napkin to blot her eyes. *Do not cry here. Not now. Save it.*

Lowering her hand, she saw a tall, male figure out of the corner of her eye. She turned expecting her date.

Nicholas.

She couldn't breathe. Was this her imagination?

"Hi, beautiful."

It *was* him.

She jumped from her seat, the chair nearly crashing backward to the floor. She swung her arms around his neck and held on tight. "Oh my God."

Then, the tears fell. Weeks of sorrow and pain, all

detonated in a split-second. Weeks of trying to keep it together, when having him in her arms again was all she wanted.

When Nic heard Cat crying, he almost released her to look at her face. Had he done something wrong?

But she held on, so he did too. "Shh." He missed this woman, and now she was in his arms again, like she'd never left.

"Ohmigod," she repeated. "I can't believe you're here."

"I'm here." He pulled back and wiped her tears away. "I missed you." Her lips were warm against his. It felt like homecoming. His tongue and teeth devoured her lips and explored her mouth. He couldn't get enough.

After he had his fill—maybe a minute, maybe an hour— he released her and offered her the chair. He sat next to her and clasped her hand above the table.

"I... how did you find me?"

Before he could answer, a water was placed before him and the waiter asked if he could get them a drink. Nic didn't need any interruptions. "Do you happen to know what you'd like?" he asked Cat.

"Um, the eggplant parmesan please."

He looked up at the man. "Two salads, two eggplant parms, and a bottle of Chianti Classico Riserva."

The man smiled and, taking his cue, left them in peace.

Nic turned back to her. "Celeste. I found her through

your social media. I had to make sure you didn't get back together with your ex, or whatever. When she told me you missed me too, I knew it was safe to come."

"Ohmigosh. I'm gonna kill her." Her smile betrayed her harsh words.

He wanted to laugh at how precious she looked. She wore a summer dress he recognized from Saint Lucia, dangling earrings, and her bun had a live flower in it. "I like the flower." It reminded him of their island trip.

"It was Celeste's idea. She said that's how my blind date," she made air quotes, "was going to know it was me." Cat held his gaze a moment longer, as if on the verge of saying something big.

He started instead to make sure she understood. "I'll get right to the point. I've missed you. Terribly. And I want us to figure this out." He motioned a finger between them. "I want us to find a way to make this work. Are you open to that?"

"Yes. No. God, I don't know."

His heart nearly stopped. "What don't you know?" He hadn't considered this could backfire on him.

To hell with that, he would fight for her, if necessary.

"You're a Mr. Fixer. I was broken, but I'm not anymore. How will I keep your interest?" Her eyes pleaded with him to convince her that there was more between them. More that they could actually build a life on.

"You're broken? Aren't we all broken?"

193

She blushed. "I wasn't adventurous—you brought that out of me."

He cupped her hand between his. "I didn't do that. You did that. You did only what you wanted to. And as much as I love everything we did in Saint. Lucia, I don't need acrobatics every time I'm with you." He leaned closer. "I love you for you."

Her mouth gaped. "You love me?"

"Yes. I'm certain of it. I couldn't get you out of my head."

She lifted a hand, stroking his cheek, then she kissed his lips softly. "Well, I love you too."

Tears welled in her gorgeous green eyes. He had no idea if he'd ever see those beautiful eyes again.

"What made you change your mind? I mean, I thought when I left Saint Lucia that was it."

He nodded. Frankly, so had he.

"I got a promotion at work."

She laid a hand over his. "Oh, Nicholas. Congratulations."

The waiter quietly laid down their salads, and after uncorking the wine, poured them each a glass and left.

"As much as I thought I wanted it, I knew something was missing." He realized his push, his competitiveness with his siblings, wasn't worth the prize if he didn't have the woman he loved beside him. The promotion meant nothing without Cat there to share it with.

She bit her lower lip.

He lifted his wineglass and waited for her to do the same. "What I was missing was you." He clinked her glass and took a sip.

"So I asked myself: if you let this girl go, what do you have to show for yourself in ten or twenty years? Maybe a thriving career, but not much else."

She shook her head. "No one to share all the highs and lows."

"That's right. No one to travel to the islands with. No babies."

Her brows lifted. "Babies?"

"Yup. If you want. Otherwise, fur babies." He grinned, and she laughed. God, he missed hearing her laugh.

Through glassy eyes, she said, "Babies are good—both kinds." As if she were suddenly hungry, she looked down at her salad and speared a cube of cheese.

He did the same. His shoulders relaxed, and his mouth watered with the first bite.

He could have her in his life, they would find a way to work things out—suddenly Nic could breathe again. Everything felt right in the world.

They chatted over their dinner, but they didn't linger.

"Come back to my place," was all he needed to hear from Cat. He flipped a few large bills off his clip and laid them on the table. He didn't want to wait for the check, and he knew he'd left more than enough to include a well-deserved tip for their waiter.

He held open the passenger car door of his rental and pulled her close. He crashed his lips to hers in a desperate, passionate kiss. He craved her lips, all of her.

Cat directed him, pointing occasionally with her free hand. Now in Austin with her, he couldn't stop touching her in some form or fashion.

The door clicked closed once they entered her apartment and she was in his arms again. He pulled off her dress; she pulled off his shirt. He barely took in his surroundings when she unfastened his pants and pushed them to the carpet. Then she kicked off her shoes, and broke their kiss long enough to grab his hand and lead him to her bedroom. More clothes dropped to the floor.

"God, how I missed you. I couldn't understand how I had fallen for you in such a short time."

His hands were on her breasts, her neck, her thighs, moving without direction but trying to find everything he'd missed those last few weeks. "Me too." He kissed and suckled her neck, making his way to her nipples, laying claim to her naked body.

"Mmm. I even looked up jobs in Orlando," she said in a pant.

That comment stopped him in his tracks. "You did?"

She nodded. "Some seemed pretty good too."

"You'd move to Orlando?"

"If you'll have me."

He grinned. "Oh baby, I'll have you. Over and over." He moved her to the bed.

She giggled and laid back.

His hands and lips roamed her torso, letting her sweet scent guide the way. Pushing her legs apart, he claimed her pussy, relishing the moan from her precious lips on the first swipe. His tongue toyed with her clit, laving and circling, bringing more blood to the swollen little nub.

She moaned again. She was close.

He stood and shed his briefs, climbing on top of her, his cock aligned right at her entrance.

"Nicki, please."

"Cat, I love you. Move to Orlando, move in with me. Be a part of my life." He pushed inside her, just as he'd done their last time together in Saint Lucia.

"Nicki, I love you too." She pulled his head down to connect their lips.

Reaching a hand between them, he caressed her clit. Just a hint of stimulation to send her over the edge. Her muscles flexed and pulled on his cock—close to detonation.

She cried out and arched her back as her orgasm spiraled through her. He loved hearing her in ecstasy.

A few more thrusts, and he shot off, spilling his seed into the woman of his dreams. Dreams he didn't even know he had or wanted. But now, he wanted it all.

He slid to the side of her and pulled her close. Their panting was the only sound in the space.

"Wow," she breathed out.

"Wow is right. And we're just getting started."

She opened her eyes and smiled. "Did you see the door to my balcony when you came in?"

His eyes widened and his eyebrows hit the ceiling. Oh yeah, this was the perfect woman for him.

The End.

THANK
You

I hope you enjoyed reading Honeymoon Hideaway!

Please consider posting a review at one or more of your favorite retailers, as well as Goodreads. Even a short review, one or two lines, can be a tremendous help and encouragement to the authors. Your review is also a gift to other readers who may be searching for just this sort of story, and will be grateful you helped them find it.

Thank you!

OTHER NOVELS BY
Mia London

Accidental Tryst

Cascade Mountain Manhunt
Runaway
Renegade

Sweet Escape Series
Dry Spell
Hot Spell
Cold Spell

Undeniable Series
Undeniable Fate
Undeniable Love

Perfect Series
Perfect Seduction
Perfect Surrender

Life To The Max

Wanton Angel *(Prequel to Life To The Max)*

Beyond Lace (Hard Men of the Rockies 4)

EXCERPT FROM
Accidental Tryst

Angie fumed. This must have been what Terri referred to as *getting ugly*. How dare Mac think he could keep the boys all summer, every summer. That news had been relayed to her that morning by her attorney. And Angie would *not* go back through her divorce lawyer. Oh no. She would handle this one directly.

She stomped off the elevator, her steps determined and sure. She debated blowing past his admin, but opted for professionalism instead. "Mimi, is my husband available?"

"Hi, Mrs. MacKey. Hang on. I'll check." The bubbly thirty-something woman picked up the phone and buzzed Mac.

Angie worked her jaw to unclench her teeth.

"He said to go right in."

Angie strode around Mimi's cubicle and pushed open the thick wooden door. She'd been to his new office only one other time, right after his promotion. The bookshelves were stacked with books, sales awards, a few momentous, and few pictures of her and the boys.

"Hey, Angie. What's up?" Mac said casually as he stood and rounded his impressive mahogany desk.

She closed the door behind her. Her eyes narrowed. "You know what's up, Mac," she uttered in a stern voice, deeper than she'd intended.

"Oh, is this about having the boys for the summer?"

He damn-well knew what this was about. He was toying with her. "Of course, it is. Why the hell else would I bother to come all the way downtown?" Her tone escalated.

He took three steps closer to her. She knew it was meant to intimidate, but she didn't move a muscle. "Look," he said, "you get the boys most of the time anyway. Now you can have your summers free."

Oh sure. He was thinking of her. *Not freakin' likely.* "You travel all the time." *Well, used to.* "How exactly is this beneficial for the boys? You think they'll enjoy just sitting around in your apartment all summer?"

He scoffed. "They will not."

"Of course they will."

"Oh, don't act like such a bitch," he growled.

Before anyone even saw it coming, Angie raised her right hand and sent it flying across Mac's cheek. The sound of the slap reverberated through the whole office. His cheek instantly reddened.

Her hands flew up over her gaping mouth and her eyes

widened. Never in their years together had she ever hit him. There had never been violence. She'd rarely hit the boys growing up either, choosing other forms of discipline instead.

"Oh, crap. I'm sorry, Mac. I didn't mean to do that," she said behind cupped hands. "Oh, my God. I'm so sorry."

He stared at her for what felt like an eternity. She could see the fire in his eyes. He took a step closer, and she stepped back. Her back was now almost touching the door.

"No, you're not," he said, his voice low and menacing.

"Yes, Mac. I . . . I lost my head. I didn't mean to slap you."

"Prove it."

Confused, her eyebrows pinched together. "What? What do you mean? How?"

He reached beside her and locked his office door. "Prove it," he said again, but his voice sounded more hoarse and . . . lustful than before. He kept his eyes trained on hers.

She licked her lips and squirmed ever so slightly.

She didn't ask again, and Mac didn't wait. He simply pointed to his desk, the other hand on his hip, looking authoritative. Sexy and masculine. "Hands on my desk."

Angie had never seen this side of her husband before. Perhaps she should be scared, but in fact, his dominance only fueled her from the inside out. Her nether parts came alive. She wasn't exactly sure what he had planned, although she had a reasonably good idea. "What?" she sounded like a timid mouse, her question a bit too breathy.

Without giving her any more time to stall, he wrapped his muscular arm around her waist and hauled her up against his body. His very rock hard body. *Oh my!*

ABOUT THE
Author

Mia London loves to write.
After reading fiction for years, she decided it was finally
time to put those images and scenes floating around in her
head down on paper.

She is a huge fan of romance, highly optimistic, and wildly
faithful to the HEA (happily ever after). Her goal is to

create a fantasy you will enjoy with characters you could love.

She lives in Texas with her attentive, loving, super-model husband, and perfectly behaved, brilliant children. Her produce never wilts, there are no weeds in her flowerbeds and chocolate is her favorite food group.

Facebook

Twitter

Instagram

Goodreads

Bookbub

www.mialondon.com

Email: mia@mialondon.com

Made in the USA
Columbia, SC
29 October 2024

44929074R00115